REASON TO BREATHE

A Town Called
Forgotten

BOOKS BY RACHEL BRANTON

Lily's House Series
House Without Lies
Tell Me No Lies
Hearts Never Lie
Your Eyes Don't Lie
Broken Lies
No Secrets or Lies
Cowboys Can't Lie

Finding Home Series
Take Me Home
All That I Love
Then I Found You

Town Called Forgotten
Kiss at Midnight
This Feeling for You
Reason to Breathe

Other
How Far
Royal Quest

Picture Books
I Don't Want To Eat
  Bugs
I Don't Want to Have
  Hot Toes

UNDER THE NAME TEYLA BRANTON

Unbounded Series
The Change
The Cure
Protectors
  Ava's Revenge
  Mortal Brother
  Set Ablaze
The Escape
The Reckoning
Lethal Engagement
The Takeover
The Avowed

Other
Times Nine

Imprints Series
First Touch (prequel)
Touch of Rain
On The Hunt
Upstaged
Under Fire
Blinded
Street Smart
Hidden Intent
Checked In

Colony Six Series
Insight (prequel)
Sketches
Visions

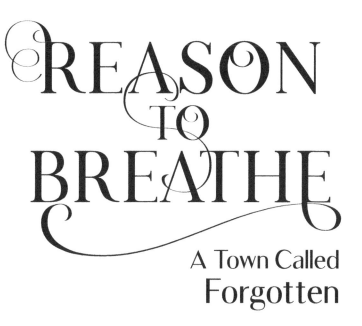

REASON TO BREATHE

A Town Called
Forgotten

RACHEL BRANTON

WHITE
STAR PRESS

This is a work of fiction, and the views expressed herein are the sole responsibility of the author. Likewise, certain characters, places, and incidents are the product of the author's imagination, and any resemblance to actual persons, living or dead, or actual events or locales, is entirely coincidental.

Reason to Breathe (A Town Called Forgotten, Book 3)

Published by White Star Press
P.O. Box 353
American Fork, Utah 84003

Printed in the United States of America
ISBN: 978-1-948982-28-3
Year of first printing: 2021

To my family for their unlimited support and love.

CHAPTER 1

Though it was barely after ten in the morning, the world outside Keisha Jefferson's small house on Third Street had grown dark. The sudden change drew her outside as if pulled by an unseen rope, even though storms weren't unusual for late September in the town of Forgotten when the weather began to shift all over Kansas. She came to a standstill in the driveway near her bright red Chevy Sonic as the first drops of rain began pelting the sidewalk.

Her accident had occurred on a day like this four and a half years ago, an accident that had irrevocably changed her life.

For the second time.

Wind tore through the trees along the street, ripping away leaves and tiny twigs and scattering them over the yard. Dust hung in the air. Her freshly combed hair whipped around her face, the dark brown strands knotting and twisting. Her eyes began to water.

Rain came down harder, like tears, and the aroma of wet

pavement filled her nose. She stood as if rooted to the spot, her thoughts tumbling. She didn't hate the rain or the driving wind any more than she hated the lightning that started the fire which had taken her parents' lives while she was still in high school. The rain simply was and holding a grudge against nature was pointless.

Still, the memories made it hard to breathe.

She remembered too vividly the rain pounding against the windshield the night of her accident and the worry that she wouldn't make it before midnight.

In the end, she hadn't made it at all.

And he had not waited.

Open the door, she told herself.

She had to be at the Butter Cake Café for work by ten-thirty, and she wouldn't get there standing by the car getting soaked. She resisted the urge to go back inside her house and curl up in bed with a cup of hot cocoa. Maggie wouldn't mind if she came in late today as the storm would most likely keep people home anyway. But Keisha would mind. Giving in to a memory was like living in fear, and she wouldn't live that way. Not now, and not ever.

She opened the door and slid behind the wheel, starting the engine with a smooth motion and checking the rearview mirror before easing out of the driveway. As she picked up speed, the rain sounded like slaps against the windshield. Goose bumps broke out across her bare arms. She should have grabbed a jacket.

She drove slowly and carefully, as she always did. It was one of the reasons she'd chosen a bright red car to replace her ruined vehicle. Everyone she crossed paths with knew the Sonic was hers, including the local police, which kept her obedient to the traffic laws. When it was raining, she made sure to keep five miles under the speed limit. These were the only concessions she'd permitted herself since accident. They were subtle and hidden, known only to herself.

She reached the north side of Main Street near the fairgrounds. Belatedly, she realized she should have gone through the back streets to avoid facing other cars in the storm, but the weather seemed to have chased everyone away. Even for mid-morning on a Wednesday, the streets were unusually deserted.

Then she saw the yellow Beetle wrapped around the huge light pole on the side of the street next to the fairground parking lot. Panic spread through her. She knew who drove that car, and no one inside it appeared to be moving.

Keisha rolled to a stop, her heart hammering in her chest. *No, not again,* she thought. Of course, it wasn't the same. This time she wasn't in that car, and no other vehicle appeared to be involved in this accident.

She hurried forward, hoping it didn't look as bad as it seemed, that the Beetle's twisted front didn't indicate a fatality—or something worse. And there was worse. She knew. Reaching the driver's door seemed to take forever, but finally, she was staring down into Laina Cox's face. Laina's shock of blond frizzy hair obscured much of her features, but her safety belt was on, and the driver's airbag had deployed. No sign of blood. Of course, that didn't mean a limb somewhere out of sight hadn't been compromised. And the way the entire front of the car was bent . . .

Keisha tried the door, but it was firmly stuck. She pounded on the side window, which was crisscrossed by myriad cracks. "Laina? Are you okay? Can you hear me?"

No answer.

She hurried around to the passenger door, seeing that the damage was much worse there. The pole blocked the doorway and took up most of the space where a passenger might have been sitting. But the door itself was half off, leaving a tiny V that Keisha could lean through into the wrecked interior. She was grateful there was no passenger.

"Laina! Laina!"

Laina still didn't move. Keisha could see now from this angle that Laina's limbs didn't seem trapped, but even awake she wouldn't be getting out from this side easily. Keisha wriggled further inside, the metal of the door jabbing into her stomach and hips as her feet left the ground. Cubed bits of glass from the shattered front window were everywhere, and she had to brush them off wherever she put a hand. At last, she reached to check Laina's pulse.

They'd gone to high school together and had even been friends at one point, but they'd drifted apart after the fire when Keisha had gone to live with her aunt and uncle before heading off to college in St. Louis. At the time, Keisha had been too numb to care, but now she violently wished she'd made more effort. She didn't know much about Laina's current life, even though they had both somehow ended up in the Forgotten Ladies Auxiliary at the request of the older members who had begged for more energetic help.

The faint jumping of Laina's heartbeat registered on Keisha's fingertips, and she let out a breathy sob of relief. Maybe it wasn't as bad as the twisted car indicated. Still, she needed help—and fast. There was no ambulance or hospital in Forgotten, and calling the one in Panna Creek would take too long, but all the officers in Forgotten had emergency training, and they could get Doc Sayer and his medical van out here faster than she could.

She fumbled for her phone, only to realize with a sinking feeling that she'd left it at home when she'd driven away so suddenly, mesmerized by the freak storm. Well, she'd use the emergency feature on Laina's phone. That would go to the station. She spied the strap of a purse on the floor between the dash and the pole and stretched to grab it, but her fingers didn't quite reach from this angle.

"Oh, Laina, I don't know what to do," Keisha muttered. Laina's neck didn't look contorted, but what if moving her did serious damage? No, Laina had to wake up before she tried to get her out of the car.

Biting her bottom lip, she reached out again and slapped Laina on the cheek.

"Wake up! Laina, wake up!"

Laina's eyes fluttered, and she shifted slightly. "Wh-what . . .?"

"You had an accident. But you're going to be okay." Isn't that what was always said, even when it wasn't true? Keisha distinctly remembered someone telling her after the accident that she'd be okay, as if her life wouldn't change forever.

Laina blinked a few more times before finally appearing to take in her situation. "Can you get me out?" She moved and then gasped. "Oh, my arm!" Her voice rose to a cry on the last word.

"How does your neck feel?" Keisha asked. "You shouldn't move too much."

Laina closed her eyes, moving her neck slightly before opening them again. "I'm a little stiff, but I'm okay. It's just my arm. And my right foot. I can't pull it out—or really feel it at all."

"I left my phone home, but I'll get the door open and see if I can get your purse from that side. We'll call police dispatch. If worst comes to worst, I'll drive to the station and come back for you. It's only just down the road."

"Don't leave me! Please." Laina's breath came out in short pants.

"Okay, I won't. I'm going around to the other side. I have something in my car that might help get you free."

Laina gave a faint nod. "Okay. Hurry."

"I will." Keisha pushed herself backward, shimmying out of the car awkwardly.

She jogged back to her own vehicle, shivering in the rain that didn't show any signs of letting up. Call her paranoid, but she'd bought the heavy-duty crowbar on the same day she'd bought the Sonic. The emergency workers had used both a cutter and a crowbar to get her out after the accident, and having one in the back made her feel safer. Silly, sometimes, but safer. And it had come in handy, both at the house and at the café.

The sound of a vehicle redirected her attention. Immediately, she ran to the edge of the road and began waving her arms wildly above her head. At this point, she didn't care who it was, so long as they had a phone or were willing to go for help, and anyone in Forgotten would do that. She'd even welcome Jeremy Wilson with his strong farmer arms and awkward advances. She'd tried to tell him it was her fault, not his, the fact that she wasn't attracted to him, but he never seemed to hear.

To her relief, the gleaming black truck angled in her direction. Hurriedly, she jumped out of the way, moving toward her car. She was opening the hatchback when the driver stepped from the truck into the rain. He wore snug blue jeans, a fitted navy jacket, and a baseball cap over his blond hair that curled at the edges. Even though her eyes were full of rain and tears, and four and a half years separated them, she recognized him instantly. He had the same blue eyes and cleft chin. Probably the same dimples too. His blond hair was darker than it had been in high school and college—as if he didn't get out in the sun much these days—but the way it curled at the edges was oh-so-familiar.

Xander! her heart sang out exultantly. But her mouth didn't form the word. It lodged in her throat, filled with bitterness and anger, hurt and betrayal.

"Keisha?" he asked, coming toward her quickly and sounding as surprised as she felt.

She wished the ground would open and swallow her before she melted into a puddle at his feet. Or, worse, threw herself into his arms.

"Are you okay?" He reached out to touch her elbow, but she backed away before he made contact.

Questions . . . so many questions came to her lips, but she bit them all back. "It's not me. It's Laina Cox. We have to get her out. And do you have a phone? We need to call the police."

"Still no hospital here?" he asked, reaching for his back pocket.

Keisha shook her head and ducked inside the hatch to grab the crowbar.

"Wait, what are you doing with that?"

"Getting her out."

"Better not to move her yet."

Fury waved over her. As if he had a say in anything she did. "I'm getting my friend out of that car," she growled, shoving back a wet chunk of hair that had fallen over her shoulder.

Turning on her heel, she hurried back to the driver's side of the Beetle. Laina was staring out the window, her face drawn with pain, looking starkly pale against the bright makeup she always wore. Her reddened lips moved, but with the noise of the rain and the glass separating them, Keisha couldn't understand anything.

She searched the door, trying to find a cranny to shove in the crowbar, but the door was pressed too tightly against the rest of the frame. Giving in to a moment of frustration, she banged on the side of the door with the palm of her hand.

Xander came up next to her, his phone in hand. "Let me see if I can push it open from the other side. I need to assess her anyway."

Before Keisha could respond, he was around the other side of the car, trying to squeeze through the V in the door—utterly impossible, given his size. Only his head and one of his arms fit. "Don't worry, Laina," he said, his voice muffled but carrying through the glass. "We're going to help. Try to stay calm. How are you feeling? Can you breathe okay?"

Keisha couldn't hear Laina's faint response, but he appeared satisfied.

More questions followed. "Can you see okay? Are you dizzy? Are you nauseated? Okay. That's okay. Can you open your eyes and look at me? I need to see them. It's going to be a little bright." And he was shining a light in her eyes like some kind of doctor.

He was back around the car in a minute, his phone pressed to his ear. "I think she might have internal bleeding," he was saying. "Doc should look at her right away. And we may need help getting her out of here, so hurry."

Keisha knew internal bleeding could be fatal—it almost had been with her. Her breathing quickened as she glanced down at Laina through the glass, fighting panic. Laina's eyes were closed again, her head resting against the back of the seat. Her right arm lay across her chest with her other arm supporting it.

Keisha lifted the crowbar in determination. She'd get the door off if she had to dismantle it piece by piece.

"Woah, there." Xander grabbed the crowbar, holding it steady but not taking it from her. "I think this outer handle is broken. Maybe you could go around and try to reach the inside one. I can't fit inside, but I think you can. And then you can push while I pull. We just need a crack."

For a heartbeat, she resisted, gripping the crowbar as if it were a lifeline in the sea of her emotions. Then she let it go, nodding shortly before hurrying around to the passenger side once more. She squeezed into the narrow space, wiggling and pushing. Pain registered on the front of her thighs, but she didn't care. Something caught—was it clothing?—and she gasped out a quiet sob of frustration because she couldn't quite get past the steering wheel to reach the door handle. Glancing at Laina's face, now a foot from her own, Keisha saw that her eyes were open and staring.

Was she dead? The wail of a police siren cut through the sound of the rain. *Please hurry,* Keisha begged silently.

Laina's eyes blinked. "Thank you," she whispered.

"You're going to be okay," Keisha responded.

If only she could crawl a bit further inside. She strained, jerking herself forward like an inchworm. Something gave way, and she lurched forward, her fingers grazing the door handle.

"I got it!" she called, giving the handle a triumphant tug as Xander pulled from the other side.

The door budged only slightly, but he pushed the crowbar in, and the bent metal creaked loudly as it opened. In the next instant, Xander was on his knees, his hands running over Laina's neck and head and then shining a light into her eyes again.

"Look right at me, Laina," he ordered. "That's it. Does your head hurt?"

"Some."

"Do you know your name?"

"Of course I do." She sounded irritated.

"You know what year it is?"

"Duh." She squinted at him. "Who are you?"

"I'm Xander Greenwood. Don't you remember me from high school?"

"Not really. You play football?"

He laughed. "Didn't most of the guys? Yeah, I played, but only because we didn't have enough better players. I'm not surprised you don't remember me. I'm a few years older than you ladies."

"Sorry," Laina said.

"Truthfully, I don't remember you either. Keisha told me your name."

Laina gave a slight snort. "Story of my life. So am I okay?"

"Well, assuming you really do know your name and the year, I like what I see now that I'm close enough to get a better look at you. You've probably broken your arm, and I think you have some minor internal bleeding we'll need to keep an eye on, but aside from some really nasty bruises on your face where you hit the airbag, yeah, you're going to be okay. But tell me immediately if anything starts to hurt worse, okay? Or if you have any new or worsening symptoms."

He sounded calm and confident, and Keisha's pulse began to slow.

Xander looked past Laina, pinning Keisha with his gaze. She was still spread out, her legs wedged in the V of the opening, her body curled around the car debris caused by the intruding light post, and her head nearly reaching the steering wheel. "You need help?" His mouth twitched as if trying to hold back a smile.

She became aware of the way her blouse drooped in front, probably giving him an eyeful of her boring grandma sports bra and her very wet, dripping hair that was straight at the bottom and wavy on top since she'd stopped the chemical straightening. She must look a laughable sight with her legs dangling through the broken car door and her hands on the edge of Laina's seat as if ready to perform some kind of strange push-ups.

Who was there in Forgotten to care anyway?

Apparently Xander, who had miraculously reappeared in her life after being missing for four and a half long years.

"I got it," she said, pushing herself backward. Pain shot through her legs.

"I can't move my foot," Laina said.

Keisha was relieved when Xander pulled his gaze away from her and looked downward. "Let me check that out." He bent, crowbar in hand.

Keisha quickly adjusted her top. If only she could find a way to back out . . . but no, she was very thoroughly stuck. And with Laina between her and the driver's side door, she wasn't going forward. Was that gas she smelled?

The sirens were close now. *Took their sweet time,* Keisha thought bitterly. The station was barely down the road on Main Street.

The metal of the car groaned as Xander put pressure on the crowbar. "Can you pull your foot out now?" he asked Laina.

"Yeah, thanks."

"I think your boot might have saved you some broken bones," Xander added. "Doesn't look too bent."

"My foot's throbbing like my arm."

"Does this hurt?" Xander moved the boot back and forth, and Laina gasped.

"Better leave it on for now," Xander said. "Turns out it boot might be better looking than useful."

"Like most men I meet," Laina muttered. "Present company excepted, of course. But the boot should have helped. It's standard issue at the hardware store, and my dad's the owner. He insists we all wear them for safety, and if there's one thing my dad knows, it's safety."

That was the moment Keisha was sure Laina would be okay,

or at least make it until Doc Sayer arrived. And if anyone could save a person, it was Doc.

A police car came to a screeching halt amid a spray of gravel, and out jumped the police chief himself, Caleb McColl. "How's she doing? I sent Levi to give the doctor an escort."

That explained why a siren was still howling somewhere in town, and the police chief was alone. McColl was a big, brown-haired man with a perpetually red face. He carried a hefty, battery-operated Jaws of Life in his big hands, which wasn't a surprise as the police and fire station were one and the same in Forgotten.

"She's doing all right." Xander adjusted the cap on his head. "Pretty sure we've got a few broken bones here, though, and Doc needs to check her out for bleeds."

Caleb bent into the Volkswagen to see for himself. "You okay, Laina?"

"I've been better," she replied.

"I'll say. You must have been going ninety to hit the pole like that. Don't you know better than to speed in the rain?"

"I swear, it wasn't my fault, Chief. The car just sped up like the gas pedal stuck!" Laina glanced over at Keisha, whose arms were beginning to hurt. "You believe me, don't you?"

"Sure." But Keisha said it only to placate her. Laina was a big prankster, and everyone in town knew it. Or at least anyone who'd gone to high school with her. Still, breaking laws wasn't something she was known to do—her daddy would have tanned her hide.

Keisha gave up on getting out the way she'd come in. Twisting, she pulled herself further into the Bug until she rested one hip on the seat. Her feet were still hanging through the opening in the door, but once they got Laina out, she'd be able to pull herself past the jutting metal, into the driver's seat, and out the driver's door.

Chief McColl nodded at her. "Good job here, Keisha. Thanks for stopping." He straightened and eyed Xander. "Don't I know you? Yeah, I do. You're Jim Greenwood's grandson, aren't you?"

Of course, the chief would recognize Xander. He'd been the chief of police for more than fifteen years, and he knew everyone in town, especially the youth. Xander had grown up here, same as she had. Though Forgotten was a small town, they hadn't run in the same circles, not in age or economic level, at least not back then, but that wouldn't have made a difference to the chief. Or, if anything, he would have kept a firmer eye on Xander, who'd had a lot more reason than Keisha to act out.

"Sure am." Xander rocked back on his heels, one hand in his pocket, the other still holding her crowbar. His body looked exactly the same as it always had, at least from her awkward position. But he wasn't the man she thought she'd known at Washington University in Missouri, where they'd run into each other and fallen wildly, passionately, and madly in love—or so she'd thought.

"You back here to take care of his place?" The chief asked. "I heard the city took it over since your mother doesn't seem inclined."

"Yeah. Sorry about the delay. I'll get it done."

"That's all right. Land sakes, looking at you makes me remember your grandpa when he was young. Man, I miss that guy."

"Me too."

Keisha heard the longing in Xander's voice, and it reminded her of so many things. The day he told her about his grandfather's heart attack for one. Or how he had looked at her when she'd talked about going home to pack a few things during spring break so they'd be ready to run away together when the semester ended.

As if.

Keisha was beginning to feel claustrophobic as another police car and a battered white van pulled into the fairground parking lot, coming around on the other side where there were no cars. When the siren cut off, they heard only the sound of the rain, and the anxiety in Keisha's stomach cranked down a notch.

Officer Levi Hughes came hurrying over, wearing his customary cowboy hat, followed by Doc Sayer, who sported a green rain jacket with the hood pulled completely over his brown hair. He pushed through the others. "I hope you didn't move her."

"I believe she's fine to move," Xander said. "No severe neck trauma. I suspect a fracture of her right forearm and possibly a break in her right foot, though the boot might have saved her from that. I'm worried about a head trauma or internal bleeding, but she's lucid, so I think it's not urgent."

Doc shined a light in Laina's eyes and then poked and prodded her until she started complaining. "Right," Doc said to Xander. "I don't know who you are, but I concur with your diagnosis."

"This is Jim Greenwood's grandson," Chief McColl said. "You might have delivered him a couple dozen years back."

Doc's gaze ran over Xander's face. "Probably been more than that, and he's changed a bit since then. I don't think his momma believed in regular medical care."

"She couldn't afford it," Xander said with an easy smile. "And a midwife delivered me."

"Sounds about right," Doc said. "Don't know how I'd get along without a midwife in town. Well, let's get Laina to my van. I've got a bed in there I can strap her to. I'd bring it out if it weren't raining so hard." He looked at Levi. "Can you come with us and drive? I'd rather her not be alone. And someone better call her family. But please tell them we don't want them all to come. Just the parents. Their clan would fill up my whole clinic."

"I'll have dispatch call her parents and send them over," said Chief McColl. "Unless you need to take her to the hospital in Panna Creek."

"I don't think so. But I'll do a few tests and X-rays to make sure. Levi, can you carry her to my van?"

Levi started forward but skidded on the unpaved parking lot.

"Darn it all, Levi." Irritation filled the chief's voice. "How many times have I told you that cowboy boots aren't a part of the uniform? This is why."

"How was I to know it was going to rain?" Levi protested. "It was clear as a bell this morning when I came on shift."

The chief snorted. "You came in before sunrise."

"Oh, right." Then lowering his voice, he muttered, "You weren't supposed to be in today, I thought."

Keisha nearly laughed at that. The chief had banned cowboy boots from the precinct after one of his officers slipped during a foot chase in the rain, but Levi bucked the protocol so much that the whole town was aware of his little rebellion.

"Be sure you don't ask me why you'll be on weekends for the next month. Now move out of the way." Chief McColl reached in to carefully scoop Laina from the car. She hissed in a sharp breath as her arm shifted, but she didn't cry out. The chief strode toward the white van with Levi and Doc hurrying after him.

Keisha struggled to pull herself through the narrow gap into the driver's seat. The steering wheel's current bent position wasn't helping matters. Xander leaned the crowbar against the car and squatted, looking at her with one brow arched. Rain dripped off the brim of his hat, and drops of rain beaded on his jacket, but otherwise, he looked completely untouched from this interlude while she suspected that she looked like something her cat had dragged in from the neighbor's garbage can.

"Need a hand?" he asked, grinning.

Before she could respond, he reached in and dragged her out as easily as the chief had lifted Laina, who was a good deal shorter than Keisha. His touch felt warm and familiar and wonderful. Quick tears came to her eyes, and she was grateful for the rain that masked her response.

The instant she was on her feet, he let her go. Too soon. And yet she knew it was for the best. Their story was over and done with, and his appearance in Forgotten had nothing to do with their relationship.

"Thanks," she said, her voice almost inaudible.

He shrugged off his jacket and draped it around her shoulders. The material was light but obviously impervious to water, and the warmth of his body lingered on the lining. He now stood in a blazing white T-shirt that was quickly darkening under the onslaught of rain.

"You keep it," she protested.

He held up a hand. "What kind of man would I be to let a woman shiver in the rain?"

Keisha stared down at the drops of rain that slicked the skin of her own hands, now clutched tightly in front of her where the jacket didn't cover them. They stood out, the color of rich honey, compared to his paler ones. "My car's just over there. I don't need the jacket."

"Please. I'll get it later." He pulled out his phone. "Is your number still the same?"

The sensation of déjà vu made her feel dizzy. He'd asked for her number when they'd run into each other that first time at

Washington University. She still had the same number, but she wouldn't tell him. She didn't want to hope for his call or an explanation of the past.

She didn't respond, and the tension that had been present all along intensified. Had the world stopped moving? Why could she no longer hear the rain?

"I'll leave the jacket at the Butter Cake Café," she choked out. "You remember it, right?"

He nodded slowly, his gaze holding hers. Was that disappointment in those blue eyes? Good. It was better than he deserved. He was a lying, betraying jerk, and she wouldn't ever let herself forget that.

"I gotta go. I'm going to be late." She turned and hurried back to her car, starting it and driving away. When she glanced in the rearview mirror, he was still staring after her exactly the way he had done four years ago in St. Louis.

"Why did you come back?" she muttered.

Yes, there were harder things than being dead.

CHAPTER 2

Keisha wandered through the back door of the Butter Cake Café like a sleepwalker. Surely this was a nightmare from which she'd wake up, and it wouldn't have happened at all. Laina wouldn't be injured, and Xander Greenwood would still be wherever the lying creep had been these past four years. Probably in Africa.

The thought pierced her heart like a knife.

Maggie Tremblay, the café owner and Keisha's friend, was standing over her big stove. She gasped at the sight of her. "What happened to you? You look like—"

"Something my cat dragged in," Keisha said miserably. "I know." She sat at the small table against the wall where employees took their breaks when they didn't want to be interrupted by customers, shrugging off Xander's jacket that somehow was still around her shoulders.

Maggie grabbed a dishtowel from a top cupboard and began drying her hair. "Did your car break down?"

"No. Laina had an accident." The story tumbled from her mouth of its own accord in ugly detail, but she found herself glossing over Xander's appearance.

Even so, Maggie latched onto his name. "Wait, you mean Xander Greenwood? Alison Greenwood's son?" Maggie pursed her lips in thought. "I wonder if he's back because of the house."

"I think so."

"So, is he a doctor now? I mean, from what you say, he seemed to know what to do for Laina."

"I don't know." Why did it hurt so much that she didn't know? There had been a time when she and Xander were inseparable, and she'd thought she knew everything about him—which was ridiculous. Who could know everything about someone after dating for only six months? Yes, he'd always been interested in medicine, but his degree had been in physics. At first it seemed an odd match for her, an economics major, but both degrees had worked well into their plans.

Sudden plans that had all gone up in flames with her accident and his betrayal. Keisha shut her eyes, fighting the urge to weep on Maggie's shoulder.

"How awful," Maggie said, giving her a hug. "I'm guessing that seeing the crash brought back a lot of bad memories."

"It wasn't the crash." The words escaped her mouth before she could help them.

Maggie settled into the chair next to her. "What then? You seem really . . . spooked. Is it something else? Does it have anything to do with why you're taking that chemistry class? You are the best employee I've ever had, but I'd be lying if I didn't say I've been wondering why you're still here after three years. I thought you'd have gone back to finish college and then on to your law degree."

Which was what everyone had expected—for her to follow in her father's footsteps. But the numbness in her heart hadn't left her after the accident, and until recently, she couldn't make herself do anything but survive.

What Maggie said about her being the best was true, and it was safe here. She knew how to be friendly and helpful while at the same time avoiding the male customers who kept pressing for her phone number. It wasn't that she hadn't dated. She'd gone out with a lot of men, especially her first year here, but none of them held her interest, not even the handsome new attorney in town. He only reminded her of the old life she had thrown away for love.

Maybe it wasn't too late, though. She'd loved the law once, or the idea of it. She could still help people and please her aunt, who, despite her snootiness, did seem to want the best for her. But even the thought of law school made her feel as if she were going backward, not forward. Thus, the chemistry class as she searched for an entirely new career, one that didn't deal with economics, the law, or crazy plans in Africa.

"The chemistry class was a mistake," she admitted. "I study and study, but I'm barely making a B grade."

"That's not too shabby."

"It is if you're Olivia Jefferson Campbell."

Maggie laughed. "Your aunt has her own challenges. You have to do what's right for you."

"Not chemistry, that's for sure. I'm mean, I'm glad I'm learning it, but it's not a subject that consumes me." Keisha picked up the towel Maggie had abandoned on the table and blotted her neck under her hair, where more water leaked down her back.

"What *does* consume you?"

Regrets, she wanted to say. *Regrets that I ever met Xander . . .* and yet that wasn't entirely true. For those brief months, she'd been wildly happy and secure in his love. Even if it had been too good to last, she'd experienced something amazing. Her time with Xander had reminded her of what her parents had found with each other. Though they had died before they passed the test of time, she was sure they would have made it. Yet she and Xander hadn't passed any sort of test, and for all the dislike Keisha felt toward her aunt, she owed her big time for helping her see Xander's real nature. Unfortunately, her time with Xander set a very high bar for any future relationship, and so far no one else had measured up.

"I don't know what I want," Keisha said, "but I like organizing and making things run smoothly." She had loved studying economics for just that reason. So maybe it was only law school that had her balking.

"You're good at that. But you need to do it on a larger scale than here with me."

Keisha gave her a smile. "I know, and I think I'm ready. I just need to decide what direction to go." Over the past year, without telling anyone, she'd finished other classes online, many in her old major. She thought she'd chosen them because they were on her economics major list rather than for any vestiges of love she had for the subject, but they were interesting, and she always came away with the highest marks in each class.

"I've actually thought about going into politics like my uncle," she added when Maggie appeared to be waiting for more. Josiah Campbell was the mayor of Forgotten, and Keisha admired him as much as she had her father. Marrying him was the best thing Aunt Olivia had ever done, though it didn't seem to be ending well for them. "I've wasted so many years, though, and it all seems a little daunting."

"The one thing about Forgotten," Maggie said with a smile, "is that no one cares where you've been. It's only where you're heading that counts."

Keisha wondered if that went for Xander too, and if he ended up sticking around Forgotten, would it make her safe haven here unbearable? How would her loved ones treat him if they knew what happened between them—or if they knew her aunt had been right about him after all?

"Besides," Maggie added. "These years haven't been wasted. They provided experiences, which I believe are more important than what you learn in any college." She paused before adding, her eyes dark and kind, "But are you sure there isn't anything more that's bothering you? Is there anything I can do to help?"

Keisha was tempted. She'd told Maggie about the boy she dated in college and hinted at a rough breakup, but she'd never told her it was Xander. Only Olivia had known—and that had been a mistake. But Maggie wasn't Olivia, and Keisha trusted her.

"It's just—" She broke off as Maggie's new husband, Garth Dalton, sauntered into the kitchen from the direction of the dining room. He was tall, dark-haired, and gorgeous, a Lieutenant Colonel recently retired at barely forty from the Air Force. He and Maggie had first fallen in love eighteen years ago before he shipped overseas, but they found each other again when a song Maggie performed at their friend's wedding had enjoyed a brief trending online. They'd been back from their honeymoon only four days.

"Hey, ladies." He bent over and gave his wife a lingering kiss. To Keisha, he added, "How are you this soggy morning?" Then he did a double take. "Ah, I see you've already been dancing in the rain, and you didn't even invite us."

Keisha forced a laugh. "I was crawling around in it, you mean." She sighed. "Anyway, there's still a lot of rain out there if you want to give it a try."

Garth laughed. "Only if Maggie comes with me." The love in his expression was like a physical stab to Keisha. Once Xander had looked at her that way.

Or had it only been in her imagination?

She pulled herself from the chair. "Well, I'd better get started on the butter cake," she said to Maggie. "If you haven't made it yet, that is."

"We might not need more if this storm keeps up." Maggie popped to her feet with considerably more energy. "Hopefully it'll blow over in a day or two, or we'll have to cancel the Harvest Festival." She made a face. "Ronica Wilson would have a breakdown. She's worked so hard, and it's all that's been keeping her . . ." Maggie didn't finish, but Keisha knew. Sooner or later, Ronica would have to face the fact that her husband's dementia was becoming impossible to manage on her own.

"It had better blow over," Keisha agreed. "People still talk about the terrible drought of sixty-six when they last canceled it."

Maggie shook her head ruefully. "Right. Superstition is a self-fulfilling prophecy."

The Harvest Festival was bigger than the Fourth of July in Forgotten. With so many of the nearly four thousand residents depending on farming and ranching, the harvest was not only important but vital to the town. It was always held the last Saturday in September, close to the time of the harvest moon. A group organized by the Ladies Auxiliary dressed in pioneer clothing and went singing down Main Street, collecting baskets and bags of harvest to give to the poor. Others not living close to Main would also bring donations later to the fairground, and those in need would come and freely take from the bounty. There would be harvest trading booths run by people dressed up as pioneers, and more booths selling fried chicken, bread, and pies. Hay-throwing and tug-of-war competitions were favorites of the men, while children made cornhusk dolls and wreaths or played children's games. The culmination of the night was always a reenactment of how James and Chelsea Morgan founded the town, followed by fireworks. Rumor had it that the singing and generous giving, coupled with a proper reenactment, called the spirit of Chelsea to bless the next harvest.

"Well, I guess I'll get to fixing the leaky toilet upstairs," Garth said. "I won't be getting any work done on the cabin today."

Maggie laughed. "A win for me since I've already tried to fix that toilet three times."

"Ah, but I have a secret," Garth said, winking at her. "By fixing, I meant that I managed to snag the phone number of your favorite plumber."

"Ernie Pike?"

"That's right. Apparently, now that he's retired, he'll only take certain calls, but you're on the list."

Maggie's grin widened. "He likes our gooey butter cake."

They laughed, embracing, and Keisha turned from them, an odd emptiness filling her stomach. If anyone deserved happiness, it was Maggie, but somehow seeing them together hurt more than it did yesterday.

Keisha grabbed a hairband from the basket next to the door that led into the counter area and dining room. Gazing into the small mirror there, she realized she looked worse than she'd thought. Her hazel eyes were reddened, her face oddly drawn and pale under her normal bronze. Four inches of dark brown hair near her scalp were wavy and wild, and the ten or so inches at the end looked scraggly and limp because of the water, and because there really was less hair there. Like most African American women, she'd gone through numerous styles of braids and weaves, and she even tried a few wigs at her aunt's insistence, but they had all resulted in pulled hairs that threatened to make her bald. By the beginning of her third year in college, she'd resorted only to straightening, but she let that go entirely this summer because straightening was turning out to be every bit as damaging. Which was why she looked like a paper doll with hair changed partway through, as if the half of her that was black battled with the half of her that was white.

Silly. She shook the thoughts away and began wrestling with her hair. It took four attempts to force the locks into a decidedly wet messy bun that at least got the mass off her neck, but she still looked rather terrible.

Maggie came up behind her. "I love your hair like that, but you don't need to put on a brave face. Why don't you take the day off? You could even go upstairs for a nice hot bath and hang out here until the rain stops. The guest rooms are empty except for the one Cora's in." Cora was Garth's troubled stepdaughter from his former marriage, and she was staying with him here until her mother relocated to Panna Creek.

Keisha turned her back on the mirror. "I think I'd rather work as long as there is something to do."

"We've got plenty to do. I need to make up more reserve bread to put in the freezer since you guys used everything when I was gone. And I really need to pin down a new vendor for strawberries. I had to throw away half of the last order. They gave us credit, but that was the third time we've had this issue, so I think we're last on their list. It's really too bad we can't get them locally."

"Okay, while you're doing that, I'll restock everything and take care of any customers. And also make at least a few butter cakes. People are bound to come in and gossip once they hear about Laina's accident. The rain won't stop that."

Maggie laughed. "You're probably right. Better change then. Did you leave your bag in your car?" Her eyes dipped to Keisha's shirt. Keisha looked down, for the first time realizing that her shirt was a blue V-neck instead of the white blouse Maggie required at work. Had she been that out of it when she left home?

"Oh no, I didn't bring one. It's been a crazy morning."

"That's okay. You can use one of mine since I just pulled a fresh batch from the dryer. They're hanging up in the laundry. I didn't have time to take them upstairs yet."

"Thanks." Keisha nodded at Maggie and Garth and ducked from the room. In the laundry room near the back entrance, she tried to reach for her phone to call Doc's office but then remembered she'd left it at home. Well, it was better to give him more time to work on Laina anyway.

In the laundry room, she found a white blouse and shut the door to change into it. Her jeans were ripped above one knee, but it was on the left, not her scarred right leg, so the skin it exposed wasn't a big deal. She grabbed a yellow apron and was heading back to the counter when the bell at the back entrance rang. She turned to see Ronica Wilson coming in with her husband, Fletcher, in tow.

"Hey," she said. "Good to see you. But I thought you guys would have come and gone already this morning."

"We should have." Ronica set her open umbrella down by the door so it could dry. She was a slender woman with short brown hair, blue eyes, and an indomitable spirit—a real force of energy.

Even if she was always in everyone else's business, Ronica was one of the kindest people Keisha knew.

"Fletcher said a big one was coming." Ronica looked fondly at her husband, who seemed much older than her fifty-odd years, though Keisha suspected that was because of the early-onset Alzheimer's disease that ravaged his body.

Keisha tied on her apron as she resumed walking. "I hope this doesn't mean we'll have to cancel the Harvest Festival."

"Nope, we won't," Rhonda said confidently, walking with her. "I'm not worried one little bit. When Fletcher told me about the storm last night, he said it would blow over by Friday morning. We might have to wait until late afternoon to start setting up, to let some of the rain soak out of the field, and maybe put down boards in some places, but it's got pretty good drainage, and Fletcher is never wrong about these things."

Keisha looked at the old man doubtfully. He was hunched over in a black rain jacket that looked far too large for him, muttering something under his breath. Today, his completely white, curly hair resembled a mad scientist from some old movie. They'd definitely been out in the storm.

"Oh, I know." Ronica smiled wistfully. "You don't know it by looking at him, and he doesn't remember it himself, but he could always foretell the weather, and he still can when he's lucid. I'm just glad Jeremy planted our corn early enough that we were able to get it all harvested. Those who aren't so lucky will have to wait for the fields to dry. Or dry the kernels after, and you know that's an added expense."

"That is lucky," Keisha said, stifling a shiver.

"Are you okay?" Ronica reached out and touched Keisha's bare arm, stopping her from walking further. "Why, you're freezing.

Is your hair wet?" Before Keisha could reply, she nodded. "Oh, that's right, you're the one who found Laina."

Keisha blinked at her. Ronica always knew everything in town, but this was uncanny. "How did you know?"

"We were at Doc's when the police called. We watched him grab his supplies and run out to his van. He even had a police escort. So of course we waited for them to come back." Ronica took her husband's arm to urge him around the bend in the L-shaped dining room. "But you don't have to worry. Laina will be all right. She has a fractured arm, a severely sprained foot, and a little whiplash, is all. I saw the X-rays myself."

"But I just barely . . ." No, Keisha hadn't barely arrived at the café. She'd spend long minutes out in the parking lot, shivering under her car heater, pounding her head against the steering wheel, and muttering at her bad luck to have run into Xander that way.

She shook the thoughts from her mind and slipped behind the counter. "No bleeding inside her head?"

"She has a pretty nasty bump on the side of her head, and there's obviously bleeding there, but Doc doesn't think it's serious enough to transport her to Panna Creek. This time anyway. But what if Laina had needed to go to the hospital? Every year, I tell the city council we need to fix the drainage along the road to Panna Creek. With the town growing, it's more important than ever. I think we need to do a series of fundraisers if we can't find the money for it in the budget." Ronica let out a frustrated breath. "Anyway, Doc's keeping Laina at the clinic today for observation, and she'll have to go home with her parents tonight."

Keisha smiled. "She's going to love that."

"I know. I told her she could come home with me, but she said her mother would never let her hear the end of it."

"Right. Well, I'm glad you told me. I was going to call and ask about her. But if you were visiting Doc . . . I mean, I hope you both are feeling well." She gave Ronica a sympathetic glance, which the woman didn't notice since she was helping her husband up on a stool. That was a decided change in his agility.

"Oh, we're fine. It's just that Fletcher's losing weight, and he's sleeping a lot. He forgets to eat these days. I wanted to make sure there wasn't a physical reason—besides his dementia, that is. Doc says no, and that I should encourage him to eat like you would a . . ." She didn't finish the sentence, but it hung there between them: *child.*

"Well, you've come to the right place," Keisha said, forcing a brightness she didn't feel. "There's nothing like a good meal at the Butter Cake to fatten someone up. Can I get you both breakfast, or would you prefer an early lunch?"

"I'd like a fruit plate," Ronica said. "I ate breakfast, but let's get Fletcher the whole breakfast deal." She smiled at her husband. "You'd like bacon, right?" To Keisha, she added, "And to think a month or so ago, I was urging him *not* to eat the bacon. Now I don't want to deprive him of anything. He doesn't understand about heart blockage and all that."

Fletcher twitched suddenly and looked at Ronica. "Cinnamon toast. I want cinnamon toast!"

"Absolutely," Keisha said. "I'll bring that to you now before I make the rest of your breakfast, okay?"

Fletcher grinned and jerked his head forward three times like a chicken in a farmyard—or maybe an excited little boy.

"Thank you." Ronica's voice held a hint of weariness now.

Keisha hurried to get the toast, giving it an extra sprinkle of sugar and cinnamon. Only a few weeks ago, Fletcher had made a huge scene in which he had broken dishes and nearly doused Maggie with a pitcher full of hot coffee, all because he wanted cinnamon toast like his mother used to make for him.

It was good to keep busy because every time Keisha stopped moving, she thought about Xander, and especially the way she'd felt drawn to him. How could he still have this effect on her after four lonely years? She hated him for that.

The lights flickered, and for a moment, she thought she'd have to turn on the generator, but the lights didn't go off. Forgotten didn't have the latest electrical equipment, though, so it might only be a matter of time. She remembered how, when she was a child and the electricity went out during storms, her mother would let her light candles, and they would play board games together in front of the fire until her daddy came home to share a picnic dinner. She'd wanted those nights to never end, and now the memories were sweet, especially as they were some of the most vivid she had of her parents.

Focusing on what memories she did have of them always helped her when the thoughts of what they would never share reared its ugly head. She couldn't change the past, and she refused to inject unhappiness into the memories. Her mother and father would never want that.

Too bad the same idea didn't work where Xander was concerned. She couldn't turn off the bad memories that shadowed their breakup. Had he followed through on their dream to go to Africa?

Tears welled in Keisha's eyes, but she forced them back. She would not cry over Xander. Not again. She blotted moisture from her eyes with a tissue before washing her hands. The only good thing about today had been that she'd forgotten to put on makeup, so it wasn't all over her face.

Well, and Laina hadn't died. Keisha still had the opportunity to revive their old friendship. She should have done so before now. She vaguely remembered Laina visiting her in the hospital after her accident—before Keisha requested no visitors except her aunt, who had been insistent.

Finishing cooking Fletcher's meal, she plated and carried it out for him. At the counter, the old man had cinnamon all over his face and fingers and looked as happy as a boy making mudpies. Ronica was attempting to smooth down his hair.

"Here you go." Keisha set the plate in front of him.

Fletcher grabbed a piece of bacon with his finger. "Yum."

Keisha laughed at the simpleness of his joy. It had been the right thing to stay here and work today. She chatted casually with Ronica as she filled in the condiments, napkins, and silverware, then slipped into the kitchen to whip up a quick batch of Maggie's special gooey butter cake. There would be at least some customers coming for lunch since the construction workers for the new pasta factory and nearby homes didn't have many other options. Even if they couldn't work in the storm, they'd still need to eat.

"Well, dear, I guess we'll be off," Ronica said when the cake was in the oven and Keisha was stocking deserts in the display cases. "I think Fletcher is finished." He was drawing with his finger in ketchup he'd squeezed onto his plate, so Keisha had to agree.

"Good to see you," Keisha said. "And I have my costume in case we still do the festival."

Ronica grinned. "Oh, we'll do it. It might even be hot. You know how the heat sometimes follows the storm. Remember that heat wave we had a couple of years ago? Fletcher thinks we're in for another one."

Keisha watched the old man lick the ketchup from his fingers. "I hope he's right. It'd be perfect for the Harvest Festival."

"Either way, we need to do the founding reenactment so we'll have a good harvest next year." Ronica helped Fletcher down, and they disappeared around the corner to the back entrance and her old truck that would be waiting in the parking lot. The café was eerily still now, the pounding of the rain outside broken only by the low whine of the bread mixer Maggie was using in the kitchen. Keisha closed her eyes briefly, but all she saw was Xander.

No, she really was seeing Xander. He was approaching the front of the café, bent against the rain that was still hitting the windows in a steady rhythm. His white T-shirt was wet. With a gasp, she ducked into the kitchen.

Maggie looked up from her bread. "You need another hand out there? I didn't hear anyone come in."

"No, it's dead. Look, um . . ." Keisha's heart banged furiously against the inside of her chest. Had Xander already entered the café? Had the storm covered the sound of the door chimes? "I think I'll go home now, after all, if you don't mind. I really do need to rest."

Maggie turned from the counter, her gaze worried. "Of course. Don't worry about anything. But are you sure you don't want to lie down upstairs?"

And pass Xander? she thought. *Not on your life.*

"To save yourself from driving, I mean." Maggie's concern leaked through her words, and Keisha felt a rush of gratitude toward her friend. Maggie might be from a different generation, but she understood trauma and pain only too well—and that didn't have an age limit.

"I'll be okay," she said, fighting to speak past the lump in her throat. "As long as you're okay with the lack of help."

"If we have a rush, Garth can pitch in. He's just gone to the hardware store for some things he needs. And Cora will be here after school."

By then Maggie could also call in one of their other two part-time high school kids. Normally they were busy enough that Maggie wanted to hire an extra person during the day, and Keisha had given her a short list of applicants after placing an ad in the local paper. But with Garth here to always lend a hand and Cora working in the afternoons, Maggie hadn't gotten around to hiring anyone yet. Keisha didn't blame her. A new husband and stepdaughter were enough changes for anyone to deal with in the short term.

"Okay then." Keisha was almost to the kitchen's back door when she remembered Xander's jacket. "Hey," she said, gesturing casually to the small table, "that jacket belongs to Xander Greenwood, if he happens to come in. He lent it to me at the accident, and I told him it would be here."

"Oh, okay." Maggie wiped her hands as a voice called to her from the counter. "Looks like we have a customer."

"I'm so sorry," Keisha began.

"Go!" Maggie made a shooing motion. "I got this."

Keisha ran.

She ran before Maggie knew it was Xander. Before Keisha could hear his voice again, or before he asked for her. And before Maggie or anyone else guessed what he had once meant to her.

At least she could be thankful that Ronica was no longer in the café. The woman would grill Xander until she knew everything about him, including what he'd eaten for dinner last night.

Outside, the rain was still pouring through the dark gray

clouds, the world suspended in a strange, watery twilight even though it wasn't yet noon. Keisha hurtled toward the outlet of the parking lot a little too fast for the rain, but she made herself slow down as she reached the street. She should have turned away from Main and circled around to her house. It was what she always did—come in down Main Street and go back home on Third, a nice little circle that allowed her to stop at stores on her way in and then not have any distractions on her way home when she was exhausted from being on her feet all day.

Instead, today she turned onto Main. Parked on the street, in front of the Butter Cake's main entrance, she spied Xander's truck. This time, however, a small, pale face stared back at her from the window.

A child?

Keisha's heart squeezed tightly, and now the tears came. Of course there was a child—probably a perfect child whose mother had made him forget Keisha. It was the final straw on her rotten day.

CHAPTER 3

Xander Greenwood wished he hadn't left his suitcase at his mother's in Panna Creek. He'd have been better off trying to stay at the old house here or taking one of the rooms at the Butter Cake, especially if the rain kept up. The drive to Panna Creek was only twenty minutes—at least on a good day—and his truck handled well, but he knew several spots in the road that became completely flooded if there was too much water—and there was definitely too much water today.

If it didn't stop raining soon, he'd be stranded here without a change of clothes or other supplies. Either that or drive the long way around, which would add nearly three hours to the twenty-minute trip. Better to stay overnight here.

Wait, no. He couldn't forget that he had Sammy and Lila with him because their mother hadn't been in any condition to take care of them today, and they'd missed the cutoff age for kindergarten this year. But the twins wouldn't mind going without a change of clothes or even a toothbrush, so he'd go look at his grandpa's old house and decide what to do from there. First, those tiny, ravenous beings needed food, lots of food.

"Why hello, Xander Greenwood." Maggie emerged from the kitchen with a welcoming smile. "I'm sorry I didn't hear you come in."

"Hey, Maggie," he said. "Must be the storm."

"Probably. But you're a sight for sore eyes. What have you been up to all these years?" Her voice was the same soft silk that had maintained order here when he and the other high school kids had come to hang out after school.

"Getting educated like everyone always told us we should."

"A good thing too. I heard you seemed pretty knowledgeable at Laina's accident this morning."

"Oh? Did Keisha say that?" He looked past her into what he could see of the kitchen, which wasn't much. From what he could see, Keisha wasn't there or anywhere else in the café.

"Well, not in those words, but I'm sure she appreciated the help, especially with it being a car accident and all."

"Yeah, no one likes car accidents."

Maggie opened her mouth as if to correct him about something, but she apparently changed her mind. That didn't surprise him—Maggie had a reputation for not gossiping, which had to be hard since she owned the most popular eating establishment in Forgotten. Even after ten years, he'd chosen to come here to eat over Gandolf's Ravioli Restaurant or Hot Stone Pizzeria.

But then Keisha wasn't likely to be at either of those locations, so maybe he had another motive. Why had she said to come here for his jacket anyway?

"I'd like to order some food to go," he said, sitting sideways on the seat so he could observe his truck. He'd left Sammy inside looking after a sleeping Lila, but he didn't trust either child to stay where they were told. "And I might need a room later if the road to Panna Creek is flooded. I'm going out to my family's old house to look around, but I'm not sure it's fit for sleeping over."

"It's definitely not." Maggie gave him a sympathetic smile. "I've been helping the Ladies Auxiliary look after it, as we do all the vacant homes, and it's pretty dusty. The last time I was there, I noticed a leak. I went up on the roof, hammered some plastic over it, and put a big rain barrel under the hole, but with all this rain, it might need more attention. I sent your mom a note about it."

"She's been doing poorly. She has diabetes. That's part of why I'm back—to help her manage it."

"Well, the house has really good lines and some great wood-work," Maggie said. "Your grandpa died before I came to Forgotten, but he seems to have known his stuff."

"I didn't realize you were relatively new here." Now that he thought about it, he only started coming to the Butter Cake his last two years of high school when he had a part-time job at the turkey factory and could pay for his food.

"It's been thirteen years now," Maggie said, her grin widening. "The luckiest yet."

"I bet." He grinned right back. Thirteen was Forgotten's lucky number. Everyone here knew that, and knowing the lore made him feel like a member of some kind of exclusive secret club.

"If you did a little work, you could probably sell the house to one of the new families who will be moving in when the new pasta factory is finished." She cocked her head at him, her dark eyes attentive. "Unless you plan to stay."

He laughed. "Well, I am going to be here for at least a year, but I'll probably live in Panna Creek. I'm working at the hospital there."

"Ah, I see. Is that related to the education you mentioned? Are you in the medical field?"

"Yeah, I'm a doctor." He shrugged. "Well, at least I've finished medical school. I was supposed to be doing my residency in an LA hospital, but I decided to come here because of my mother's health. You might not know this, but Panna Creek does have a very small residency program for family practitioners, which is what I plan to be, but the spots usually go unfilled. Guess not too many doctors want to settle in Timbuktu." He chuckled and added, "They aren't half bad, albeit a little behind the times. But I have a lot to learn from them before I can practice on my own."

"Still, medical school. That's really an accomplishment," Maggie said. "I can't tell you how many people wish there were a hospital here. Driving to Panna Creek in an emergency or waiting for an ambulance from there isn't always the best thing."

"Right." Those first few minutes could mean the difference between life and death. He'd learned that only too well.

"So what can I get you?" Maggie scooped up the pad and pencil lying between them on the counter.

He glanced at the menu. "I'll take a steak sandwich with fries and also two children's meals."

Her gaze went past him to the window. "Ah, so that's why you keep looking outside. I was wondering."

He chuckled. "One of them is asleep—or was. The other is watching her, but they aren't very obedient. With Mom sick, they're used to getting their own way."

"Mom? You mean they aren't your kids?"

He grinned. "I wish. No, they're my little half-siblings. Twins, Sammy and Lila. Just turned five."

"Oh, that's right. I've met them a few times when your mom comes to town." She took a step toward the kitchen. "They probably don't remember, though. It's been at least a year since I've seen her. Or maybe two."

"You might see them more often, depending on what I do with the house."

"Well, I'll—" Whatever Maggie was going to say was lost as a tall, lean man came from the kitchen carrying two shopping bags, his dark hair dripping. He kissed Maggie. "Stop," she said, laughing. "You're all wet." To Xander, she added, "This is Garth, my husband. We got married a few weeks ago. Garth, this is Xander Greenwood. He used to live here as a boy."

"Nice to meet you," the men said together.

She stepped around Garth. "I'll bring your food right away. Feel free to bring the kids in if you need to. There's no need to eat in the truck or at your house when you have the whole place here to yourself, though I'm hoping it picks up by lunchtime."

Maggie disappeared, leaving Xander alone with Garth. "It's like someone's dumping a bucket on Forgotten," Garth said, dropping a bag on the floor to run a hand through his very short hair.

"It won't last long," Xander assured him.

Before Garth could respond, Xander saw a movement in his peripheral vision. "Uh-oh. Excuse me. Looks like my prisoners are escaping." He dashed toward the door and out into the rain. Sammy was on the sidewalk with her face lifted toward the gray sky, her little hands shoved into the pockets of her baggy jeans and her mouth open to catch the rain.

"I said to stay in the truck," he told her.

"But I'm thirsty." She moved her face around as if to catch more water. "And Lila is boring."

"Am not boring," Lila said, gazing at them from the open door of the truck while rubbing her eyes. She wore a costume princess dress that looked as if she'd slept in it for a week, though she hadn't—he'd checked the smell.

The girls were identical from the tops of their white-blond heads to the tips of their stubby little toes, but in temperament and attitude, they were as opposite as any children could be.

"All right," he said. "Let's go inside and eat."

"I thought we were going to Mom's old house," Sammy said, her lower lip jutting in a pout. "I wanted to look for bones and hidden treasure."

"We are, but it might be a little too dirty to eat there."

Sammy rolled her eyes. "Mom says a little dirt never hurt anyone."

"So she does." Xander had to laugh because he remembered too vividly his mom saying the very same thing to him when he came home from elementary school after being teased by some of the bigger kids about his old clothes. It was around the time he started showering without being asked.

"I don't like dirt," Lila said, pursing her lips. "It's awful." She pulled on the hood of her pink jacket and reached for him.

"I'm wet," he warned.

"That's okay." She was like a princess bestowing her favors.

Balancing her on one hip, he slammed the car door and hurried back into the Butter Cake. He set Lila down at a table and then had to go outside again to drag Sammy into the café. He should have known better than to come today in the rain. But he was supposed to start at the hospital next Monday, so this week was all he had.

He'd also be lying to himself if he didn't admit that part of his reason for being here was because he wanted to find out what had happened to Keisha. So many times over the years he'd picked up his phone, thinking to call, but she never returned those initial calls when he tried to ask her what was going on, and her aunt made it clear that she didn't want to see him. He figured she was a big city attorney by now, but here she was on a regular workday morning, wearing jeans and driving on Main Street in this little town.

Maggie was back with the food quicker than he expected, and the little girls dug in. But the sight of Maggie returning with the jacket he'd loaned Keisha robbed him of appetite. "I almost forgot this," she said, handing it to him. "Keisha wanted me to give it to you if I saw you."

"Thanks. Uh . . ." He paused, wanting to say something before Maggie left the table again, but what? His mind raced. Was this it? Would he ever see Keisha again? Had she purposefully left his jacket here to give him the slip? His hands clenched at his side. No, she probably hadn't thought of him at all, and he wasn't going to be pathetically upset about it. That wasn't who he'd become.

"Was there something else?" Maggie prompted.

Making a decision, he said, "Yeah, I thought Keisha would be here when she mentioned the café, though I guess that's kind of silly since she probably has to work."

Maggie smiled. "Actually, Keisha normally would be here—she works for me. But with it being so slow and the accident and all, I told her to go home early." There was a slight hesitation before she added, "Being first at the scene of an accident isn't all that fun. And she was soaking wet. I was worried she'd catch a cold."

Keisha worked here? At a bed and breakfast café? That didn't seem like the Keisha he'd known. She'd been ready to conquer the world. He couldn't wrap his mind around the idea. "Oh," he said, rather lamely. "I'm sorry to have missed her."

Maggie must have sensed something in his voice because she said, "I didn't know you knew each other. She was a couple years behind you in school, wasn't she?"

Which meant Keisha hadn't talked about him. He didn't know whether to be insulted or hurt. Why did it matter?

"Older guys always notice the cute younger girls." He injected humor he didn't feel into his tone. "She was way out of my league, though." And then, because he couldn't help himself, he added, "We actually met again in college. We were both at Washington University in St. Louis."

"Oh, that's always fun. Keisha—" But Maggie broke off, as if reminding herself not to pass on gossip.

Keisha what? She'd been a good student? Finished at the top of her class? Dropped out? What? He couldn't help wanting to know.

"I thought she'd be a big-time attorney by now," he said. "That's what her aunt always pushed for."

"We all thought that, and as for Olivia . . ." Maggie smiled. "Enough said."

He agreed. If there was anyone Xander disliked in Forgotten, it was Oliva Campbell, the mayor's wife and half-sister to Keisha's father.

"Well, thanks again," he said as Maggie moved off. "Eating at the house probably wasn't a good idea."

Maggie paused. "Speaking of that, do you have a key to the house?"

He shook his head. "I was going to see if I could get in a window."

"No need. There's a key under a rock at the base of the mailbox.

Your mom left it with the Ladies Auxiliary when she moved, and we keep a copy there for when people make the rounds to check up on things. Known only to the ladies, of course. Until the kids catch on, it saves us from driving to city hall where we have a storage locker for those kinds of things."

"Smart. Thanks."

"Anytime. And if you need help with the roof, Garth might give you a hand after the rain stops. He's a retired air force pilot, and he's got time on his hands until he figures out what he's going to do next. So just ask."

"I will. Thanks." Xander had learned about fixing things himself during his last years with his mother after his grandpa died, and during the years of working his way through college, but his skills were rusty. The only thing he'd been doing the past four years was sitting with his nose in one medical book or another.

They ate in relative peace until Sammy began shooting tiny spitballs through her straw—something he would have done at her age and older, but it didn't seem funny now. "Sammy, enough!" he said.

She heaved a sigh. "You're as bad as Dad when he's home."

As their father was a long-distance truck driver, he wasn't home often enough, especially with their mother sick, but Xander was going to have a serious chat with him the next time he was in town. At least his stepfather's paycheck kept them in relative comfort, which was far more than Xander's father had ever done. That man had come through town only to help with the harvest, leaving his mother behind, heartbroken and pregnant, when he moved on. Xander didn't even know his name—or care to know. If his mother remembered, it wasn't something they talked about.

The town had talked, though, thanks to Olivia Campbell and her ilk. Xander's family had been white trash to the likes of them, even though his grandfather had been respected by all. But his mother hadn't cared about them—only about Xander— and he'd taken his cue from her. His memories of this town had been largely good, and being back here was like a balm to his soul.

Except he couldn't stop thinking about Keisha now. Seeing her was like drinking water after four years in the desert. How could she still affect him that way? Even in high school he'd noticed her beauty—he would have been blind not to. She stood out to everyone, not only because of her bronze skin color in Forgotten's mostly white community but because of her outgoing personality and friendly smile. Yet it was only in college when they met again that he dared to approach her—and had fallen totally and completely in love. She was better than his boyish dreams of her, and she had been his whole future. Or so he'd thought—until she walked away.

No, not walked—ran. Disappeared. Thinking about it opened a hole in his gut.

"I have to go pee," Sammy whined, doing a wiggling dance in her seat.

He pointed to the clearly marked sign on the café's bath-room door. "Then go." He hoped she knew how to go by herself because he didn't know anything about helping little girls use the potty.

"Me too," Lila said.

"Of course, you do. Well, go ahead." He watched them leave, hoping Sammy wouldn't clog up the sink as a joke. Sometimes her silly pranks were more damaging than they were funny.

Long minutes ticked by, and he was about to go in after them when Maggie appeared from nowhere. "I'll check on them," she offered.

"Thanks. It might save you a plumber's visit."

Maggie laughed. "Okay then."

She was back out with the girls in record time, and he didn't spy water on the floor behind them, so it was all good. "Thanks, Maggie."

"Any time. Let me know if you decide you need a room. With it raining cats and dogs, you're probably right about the road being flooded by the time you're ready to go back—if it isn't already. We've got two rooms open upstairs, if you'd rather, but the girls could sleep on a trundle in yours so you wouldn't have to pay for two rooms."

A good thing since he promised his mother he wouldn't let Sammy out of his sight. "I will. Thanks again." The large tip he left her was easily worth it. He was finally warm, and his stomach was no longer complaining.

They hurried out to the truck, with him once again carrying Lila. The rain had not let up. Sammy stopped and stared into the sky.

"Get in," he said, motioning.

"I'm trying to see the cats and dogs Maggie said were coming down."

He laughed. "It's just a figure of speech." Seeing things from a child's eyes never ceased to amaze him. When he'd been assisting in medical school, he learned that they were good at noticing the little things. He also found it amazing that their youngest patients could often endure more physical pain than the adults.

"What's a figure of speech?" Sammy asked.

He explained the concept as he drove to where his grandfather's house sat on the edge of town, close to the turkey factory.

On hot summer days it wasn't exactly the best location because of the smell, but for now, the rain was their only challenge.

He found the key and went to open the door before going back to carry Lila in. But suddenly she was all grown up and didn't need to be carried. Luckily the cobbled walkway was still mostly intact, and she wouldn't soil her princess shoes too much.

"Don't mess with anything!" he ordered as Sammy disappeared the minute they were inside the house.

"I won't," she called from some unknown location.

Which, of course, meant she would. Not that it would matter as the house had been long abandoned. His mother had moved to Panna Creek ten years ago after he left for St. Louis. He hadn't known it then, but she'd only been waiting for him to finish school so she wouldn't have to uproot him when she married Niles Tyler, the twins' father. Xander got along with Niles well enough when he came home for visits, which hadn't been very often, and his mother seemed content, so he was happy for her.

But he hadn't been a dutiful son. While he thought working his way through college was hard—it had taken him six years— he hadn't a clue about how much more challenging medical school would be. And all the while, his mother's battle with diabetes had been worsening. Well, he was helping her get it under control now so she could get back to taking care of the twins properly. Currently, they were spending far too much time doing their own thing or having neighbors check in on them.

Stepping into the house was like stepping ever further into the past. He'd loved it here, growing up with his mother and grandfather, whom he'd worshipped. Everywhere he looked, he could see his grandfather's hand, from the carefully laid wood floor and elaborate crown molding to the heavy, handmade table that still stood in the kitchen. This was home, his past, his roots.

Maggie had been right that the house had beautiful wood-work. Xander hadn't noticed as a child or teen, but he saw it now. The walls had hideous paper, and the carpeting was frayed and dirty, but the wood, the lines, and the bones of the house spoke of lasting quality because his grandfather had built it. If anyone had been around to repair the small things and update the spaces with new styles, the house would be in a lot better shape now. Not that it mattered. He was here to figure out what to do with the house, not restore it or mire himself in nostalgia.

He ran a finger along the dusty railing, a faint memory of his grandfather restaining it coming to mind. It looked like it had been done yesterday. The fireplace mantel was another work of art, and even the kitchen table, scraped and covered with dust, was amazing. Before Xander left, maybe he'd take it with him to remember his grandfather. His new apartment in Panna Creek sadly lacked any furniture except a futon where he slept. Now that he was earning money as a resident, the dearth of belong-ings would change, but slowly since he had a lot of school debt to pay.

Amazing as the wood was, the best discovery was the antique toy cars his grandfather collected. A dozen or so were still in the front room, and more filled a large display cabinet in his grand-father's old bedroom. He remembered playing with them as a child. He'd always known they would be his one day. How had he forgotten them for so long?

A crash upstairs had him hurrying to see what Sammy was up to. He found her in his old room, balancing on a stool—another of his grandfather's creations—and staring at a blue plastic box she'd obviously tried to take down from the top shelf in his closet.

"I didn't mean to," she said before he could speak.

His eyes riveted on the box. It had opened like a little suitcase, and tiny toy cars spilled out. Hundreds of them, a collection he hadn't touched for fourteen years. They were small, simple things, unlike the larger ones his grandfather had collected. He'd thought his mom would have gotten rid of them by now— either sold off at a yard sale or donated to charity—yet here they were, right where he'd left them. A strange sense of contentment welled in his chest.

"Wow," he said, kneeling on the dusty carpet to take a closer look.

"They're just cars," Lila said. She was holding up her princess dress so it wouldn't drag in the dust.

"Cool cars," Sammy corrected. "Old ones. This house is loaded with old junk. Maybe we can sell it and make a bunch of money. That's what they do on the show Mom watches."

"No one is selling any of my cars." Xander began replacing them in the slots.

"Yeah, especially because Sammy broke the box," Lila said with a sniff.

"It's supposed to open like that. See?" He showed her how it closed. "Help me get all these back in." Both girls bent willingly to the task, Lila even forgetting to protect her dress from the dirt. The girls scattered as he closed the case and set it by the door. He'd take it back to his apartment where the twins could play with them when they came over, and someday he'd have kids of his own who might like them. The idea had him smiling. He'd get a shelf for all his grandfather's cars as well, though they might be out of place in the modern space.

He hadn't seen the barrel or the leaking ceiling that Maggie had mentioned, and though that should have been his first priority, he couldn't resist looking around his room a bit more. His dresser was still in the corner—also made by his grandfather—and his twin bed frame was here, but the dresser was empty and the mattress missing, and there were no pictures on the walls. While his mother had obviously made at least some attempt to pack up the house, she seemed to have overlooked more things than she'd taken or given away.

"Uh, Xander, there's water on the carpet out here."

He looked over from the bed to see Sammy peeking back into the room. "Show me," he said. Time to get to work.

Sure enough, water was leaking from the attic door, and he showed the girls how to pull down the hidden stairs and climb up. The attic was stuffed with generations of Greenwood paraphernalia, and right in the middle was a huge rain barrel, now full of water that rippled with the steady drops still leaking through the ceiling.

"Uh-oh," Sammy said, having gone first.

Xander ducked his head as he reached the top, but there was just enough room to stand, which made him guess he was near his grandfather's height. "Look around for some buckets or plastic containers or something. We need to bail out some of this water. It's leaking pretty fast with all that rain." Sammy began digging into a box while Lila, still on the ladder with only her head above the floor, reversed course and disappeared.

He found an old, plastic cake container and filled it with water from the barrel. It wasn't big enough to make much of a dent, but if he tossed the water out the window, maybe he could lower the level enough to look for something bigger out in the shed.

"I found this!" Sammy popped up from behind a box with a small kitchen bucket. She hurried over.

She filled while he dumped, and by the time Lila joined them with a huge stainless-steel bowl from the kitchen, they had brought the water down a few inches in the barrel. He thought about asking them to find towels to mop up the wood floor, but the floor appeared well-sealed, so the real damage would be in the carpet on the floor below, which would likely need replacing anyway. He'd have to pull it up and see what was under it.

No, he'd hire someone since he had to start work next week. He blew out a breath of frustration.

Lila groaned. "Oh, I'm so tired. My arms are going to fall off."

He knew what she meant. "You guys just fill them up. I'll dump, okay?"

But it wasn't going to be okay.

"I'm going to have to go out on the roof to see if I can stop the leak," he said. "But first, I need to check if there are tools in the shed." And maybe some plastic and nails. Or something. But would the neighborhood kids have broken into the shed and taken everything? His grandpa hadn't kept it locked back then, and it might not be locked now. Resolutely, he hurried outside into the deluge to see what he could find.

Investigation showed a new combination lock on the large work shed at the back of the property. But the window was warped enough that he was able to open it and climb through. Again, he had the feeling of stepping back in time. While the aroma of dust was more prominent than wood, standing there in the dimness brought back so many memories of watching his grandfather work. Work and tell his stories about Africa and how he helped build houses and wells and taught the kids to play baseball.

Shaking himself from the reverie, Xander began pulling open drawers. A few were empty, but most had tools and screws and nails. He took the first hammer he found and filled his pockets with nails. There was no plastic, but a large scrap of wood should help, if he could get it out the window.

By the time he made it back to the girls in the attic, the water was nearly at the top of the barrel again. He bailed out more and then contemplated how he'd get onto the roof through the attic window, eventually deciding it would be suicide, even without the rain. So he ran back to the shed to find a ladder. There wasn't one, but he found a larger bucket.

Sammy rolled her eyes when she saw him. "Are you kidding? That's still not going to help much."

"It'll have to be enough until I can find a ladder somewhere."

But she was right. He could bail all day and barely keep up with the rain. What was he going to do? This wasn't exactly something they covered in medical school.

Well, he could call Maggie at the Butter Cake. She'd offered help, and he was certain she'd have a tall enough ladder or know where to borrow one.

He wiped his hands to get rid of the dirt that had formed from the dust and water before pulling out his cell phone. But the call didn't go through, and he had zero bars. The storm must have knocked out the cell tower.

He looked at the kids, whose faces were streaked with mud. His frozen mind kept thinking that once Lila realized how dirty her dress was, there were going to be tears.

What now?

Maybe climbing out the window onto the roof was his only option.

CHAPTER 4

Keisha didn't go straight home but instead stopped at city hall on Main Street next to the police station. For no reason she could define, she felt a need to talk to her uncle, Forgotten's mayor, Josiah Campbell. Since her father's death, he'd been the only real male role model in her life, and there wasn't a better one. He was in large part the reason Keisha kept working on her difficult relationship with her aunt. If anyone had words of advice about Xander, it would be him. When she arrived outside his office, the door was open, which meant he wasn't in a meeting.

"Keisha, hi," said Penny Jenkins, his very plump, gray-haired secretary.

"Can I go in?"

"Sure. He's always glad to see you, but . . . um, now that you're here . . ." She darted a glance at the door and then started again, her soft voice going even softer. "I've been meaning to call to ask if something is wrong."

"You mean about the accident?"

"Accident?"

"Laina Cox had a car accident this morning. I thought you might have heard." Keisha knew her younger daughter, Ayleen, was good friends with Laina. "Anyway, she's going to be okay. She's with Doc at the clinic. Or was."

"Oh, thank the dear Lord!" Penny looked briefly heavenward. "She's such a sweet girl."

"Yeah. But if it wasn't about Laina, what were you talking about?"

"It's Josiah," Penny said, her voice now a whisper so soft that she was practically mouthing the words. "He's not himself, and I know for a fact that he's worn the same suit for three days straight."

"That doesn't sound like him."

"No. But it's not my place to say anything. I was going to call Olivia, but you know how that goes."

Keisha didn't know if she meant that almost everyone avoided Olivia and her shrewish tongue or if Penny knew her aunt and uncle's marriage was on shaky ground. "Right," she said, deciding the answer covered both things. "I'll talk to him."

"Thank you." Penny smiled widely, her round face dimpling in both cheeks.

Pushing her own troubles to the side, Keisha strode toward Josiah's office. It wasn't as if Xander was here to stay anyway. Her uncle was more important.

He looked up with a smile as she came through the door. "Keisha, how good to see you. I was thinking about heading to the Butter Cake for lunch. What brings you here? Aren't you supposed to be working?" He stood to give her a hug.

"I am, but it's dead there because of the rain. And I got wet earlier and haven't really dried out." The shirt she'd borrowed from Maggie was already damp from simply running to and from her car.

He reclaimed his seat. "I heard about the accident. But Laina's going to be okay. It's a good thing you live out that way."

"If I hadn't found her, someone else would have." Someone like Xander.

Josiah must have sensed the hesitance in her tone. "I'm guessing it was bad, bringing up those old memories." His voice was deep and gentle.

"Yeah, not too good." Only to him would she admit it. "But let's talk about you for a minute."

"Me?" His salt and pepper brows rose high, but he didn't fool her. Josiah was a tall, muscular man with graying black hair and skin the color of midnight. Normally, he was the picture of calm wisdom and elegance, but today he looked worn and rumpled, and there was an odd pallor to his dark skin.

"Your suit is all wrinkled," she said, "and you look like you haven't slept. Is something wrong?" She paused, hands on her hips. "And before you say you're fine, I'm not the only one who's noticed."

His eyes strayed to the door. "Penny."

"Yes, she's noticed something off these past few days." Keisha took one of the heavy chairs in front of the mahogany desk and dragged it around to the side where she could be closer to him. "But to me, you've been acting different for months."

He dragged in a breath, holding it a long time in his chest before releasing it like a prayer. "It's over. With Olivia, I mean. I've known for years that it was coming, and I thought it would be a relief . . . and it is . . . but it still represents a very terrible failure."

Keisha nodded. "I'm sorry. But you have to know that you did everything you could to save your marriage—and more. I'm a witness." She'd certainly had a front-row seat to Olivia's callous treatment of this strong, gentle man.

"I do know that, but I thought . . . I was hoping we could last until Charlie was out of high school and in college. Less of a change for him. But at least Olivia has agreed not to uproot him, which will have to do."

"So you moved out?" It wasn't much of a guess because Olivia would never leave their lakeside mansion, which was the finest in Forgotten, rivaled only by city hall itself. At least she wouldn't unless she was leaving town altogether for something better. "Where are you staying? Why didn't you come to my place?"

He shook his head. "No, I'll find something, but for now, I'm staying here in my inner office. The bathroom has a shower, and there's even a closet. The couch isn't that uncomfortable to sleep on. I know it's a temporary measure, but the town's bylaws actually provide a modest residence allowance for mayors, which we've never used, so there isn't a designated house, but there are several modest properties that have reverted back to the town, so I'm looking into those now. Using the allowance will allow me to take care of Olivia and Charlie until he's in college. She'll be moving after that—she's hated this town nearly from the beginning—and I'll move back into my own house then."

Keisha knew if it hadn't been for Charlie and Josiah's utter refusal to leave Forgotten or back down on custody issues, Olivia might have divorced him and left town shortly after Keisha's parents' deaths.

"I'm sorry." Keisha shook her head. "If my parents hadn't moved here and loved it so much, Olivia never would have come, and you two wouldn't have—"

"Hush now," he said. "I don't regret it for a minute. At least not those early years, and I could never regret Charlie."

Neither could Keisha. Charlie was every bit his dad's son, with none of Olivia's bitterness and entitlement. "I'm still sorry," she said. "I know you hoped things would change."

"But I am relieved," he admitted. "I don't have my clothes or things, and I'm missing every second I don't see Charlie, but for the first time in a long time, there's hope."

She saw it then. Beneath the rumpled weariness, something new burned in his eyes. "It'll be rough at first," he added, "but the fact that this happened at all means Olivia has finally reached the point where she cares more about freeing herself from me than about the town talking."

"Good old Aunt Olivia. She always did worry about what people were saying." How her aunt could be so different from her father couldn't be easily explained. He had been four years older, and they had different fathers, but both had been privileged growing up and educated in fine colleges. Their fathers had been supportive, and their mother had loved and cared for them equally until she succumbed to breast cancer at age sixty.

"Might also have something to do with an online friendship she has developed with an old college boyfriend," Josiah said. "But I don't ask about that. In fact, I want her to be happy. Maybe we both can be." Which meant maybe he hoped he could find love again too, and Keisha knew it wasn't out of the question. He was a kind, loving man, and at fifty-two, he had much of his life before him.

"We're not really telling people," he continued. "I mean, it'll come out in a few weeks when she files for divorce—everyone knows everything in this town—but for now, we're keeping it low-key."

"You'll have to at least tell Penny. She'll keep it quiet if you ask her to. And you need to get more clothes."

"I was supposed to drive over today when Olivia went to Panna Creek to get her hair done, but with the rain, she didn't go. I find myself reluctant to be there when she is. I should have brought more initially, but I had other things on my mind."

"I'll go. Just tell me what to get. And you're totally welcome at my house. Anytime."

"Olivia would be livid if I sent you."

That was the truth, and while he wasn't a cowed man who was obedient to the wicked witch, he was a diplomatic person, and Keisha suspected keeping things cordial would be the only way he'd get to spend as much time as he wanted with his son.

"Anyway, I'm giving Charlie a ride from school to the vet clinic after school and then taking him home when his shift is over, so I'll pack up then. It'll be easier to come back here with my things after everyone's gone home for the day."

"Good thinking. Don't forget extra socks, and you'll have to take this suit to the dry-cleaners."

He gave a deep chuckle. "That's one thing Olivia always did well—made sure I looked the part. Guess I'll have to take care of that on my own now."

"I guess so. Well, I'd better get going. I'm still pretty chilled." Keisha stood, feeling both sad and happy for him. He'd endured a lot at the hands of her aunt, but failing after trying so hard was something he would have to come to terms with. At least he'd given it his all. Sometimes she wondered if she could have done more with Xander. Of course, being in a hospital for two months had killed most of her options.

"Take a hot bath and drink some herbal tea," Josiah advised.

"I will."

She left him then, pondering how he could look so out-of-sorts and yet have that spark of hope. Maybe it was the way he chose to look at the situation.

The idea struck a chord in her. Having Xander here wasn't ideal. In fact, she wanted to lock herself inside her house until she was sure he was gone, and yet . . . maybe it was time to find a way to move forward in both her personal and professional life. She'd been trying to do that with her new classes, and in large part had succeeded, but the chemistry class had been a mistake. She needed to return to studying economics as that would be the fastest way to finish her degree and go to law school. Unfortunately, law school seemed like another woman's dream now. The economics classes, she welcomed, but the rest? She wasn't so sure.

She drove home a little too slowly, but there was really no one around to see her. No, on days like this, the residents of Forgotten hunkered down by a warm fire, sipping tea and eating gooey butter cake. Or maybe Kansas dirt cake, which was also a popular town dish.

Her cat ran to her as she came into the house, rubbing up against her despite the wetness on her torn jeans. "Hey, Cupcake." Keisha picked her up and cuddled her as she went to the bathroom and turned on the water. In a few minutes, she'd be soaking in warm bubbles and drinking hot cocoa.

She was heading to the bathroom with the cocoa when the doorbell rang. She hurried to answer it but paused in front of the door. It couldn't be Xander, could it? Unfortunately, the house was too old to have a peephole, but she made a mental note to get one installed in case some other ex-love of her life happened to come into town.

She tried to run her fingers through her hair only to realize it was still up in a messy bun, which was now so bedraggled that it threatened to fall out altogether.

Of course, she thought, setting her cocoa down on the small end table near her sofa. If it was Xander, she didn't want to end up spilling the still too-hot liquid on herself. Besides, she might be tempted to throw it at him.

She opened the door, experiencing an instant of shock when instead of Xander, it was Ernie Pike, her parents' old neighbor. He'd been their plumber before he retired, and his daughter babysat Keisha when she was little. Now he only did jobs for his favorite customers. He was one of the kindest people she knew, but he had the hoof of a cow, as they said in Forgotten, which meant he was a big-time cheapskate. He borrowed far more tools than he owned, rarely went out to the movies or to eat, and fixed things around his house with duct tape. This cheapness was a bonus for his customers because he cut every corner he could without doing a shoddy job by refurbishing old fittings or buying second-hand ones, which usually meant a more economical bottom line. And his plumbing usually stayed fixed too, which was surprising given his proclivity for duct tape in other areas of his life.

"Hi, Mr. Pike," she said, curiosity getting the best of her. "Can I help you?"

He nodded his head of shaggy gray-blond hair, which she suspected he cut himself rather than pay twelve dollars plus a tip at the salon. "Good day to you, Keisha. I'm glad you're home. Well, I mean, I knew you would be since I just came from the Butter Cake, and Maggie mentioned she'd sent you home. I can't imagine how you must feel about finding your friend this morning."

Did all of Forgotten already know about her involvement in

Laina's accident? "I'm just a little chilled," she said. "I'm about to drink some hot cocoa and take a hot bath."

"Good idea. I'll get out of your way. I just wanted to borrow your ladder, if I could."

"Why, of course." Whatever he'd be doing with a ladder in this rain, she didn't even want to ask, but he was old and getting frailer, so with a little internal sigh, she said, "You're not going to pick those apples today, are you? I'd be willing to help you when the rain stops."

"Oh, no." The corners of his brown eyes crinkled with amusement. "My grandsons will take care of that, but I might as well keep the ladder for them, now that you mention it."

"Might as well."

He had the aluminum ladder more often than she did, but it had been her parents' ladder, and she wouldn't have it at all if he hadn't borrowed it before the fire. He'd brought it back when she'd finally left her aunt's house after the accident, and Keisha had been fiercely glad. She used the ladder every year to clean out her rain gutters and put up Christmas lights. Once, it even came in handy at the blackened ruins of her parents' old house, where she rescued a wooden box of mementos from the attic that somehow survived mostly intact. That was before Olivia had the place razed a few years ago to prevent the neighborhood children from playing inside and getting hurt.

"You know where it is," she told him. "Out in the carport." She had it leaning up against the house with a tarp over it until she made the carport into a garage, so hopefully it wouldn't be wet. "But are you sure you need it today?" She gestured pointedly at the wet world behind him.

"Oh, it's not for me. I was driving home after fixing Maggie's toilet, and I saw this guy bailing water out of his attic. Darn fool looked like he was about ready to climb up on the roof from the window, so I told him I'd go get a ladder." He shook his head. "Kids these days think they're Superman."

Keisha stifled a snort. "Right. Well, are you sure *you're* not planning to go out on that roof?"

"I might do so. Guy doesn't look very handy. I think he might have recently bought the old house. The man who owned it has been dead a lot of years."

Keisha began feeling her hot bath slipping from her fingers. "Well, you get the ladder, and I'll come along to see if we need to round up more help." No way was she going to let the old man slide off a roof in this rain, good deed or no.

"What about your bath?"

"It can wait."

"Get a coat on then. And don't forget to turn off your water, or we'll have another flood on our hands."

Keisha was nearly out of her regular clean clothes as she'd missed laundry day, so she changed quickly from her wet jeans to a pair of rarely-used hiking pants that were both water-resistant and quick drying. One of her last two clean T-shirts, a sweater, and a rain jacket should keep her warm and give her mobility in case she was the one who ended up on the ladder. A glance in the mirror told her there was no hope for her hair, so she simply added another elastic.

She was finished before Ernie had loaded the ladder into his old gray truck with the faded plumber advertisement on the side. He'd painted over the number on the day he retired. She knew because he borrowed Maggie's paint.

"I'll follow you," she told him, pulling her hat down further to stave off the rain from dripping into her eyes. "That way you won't have to come back to drop me off."

"I don't mind. It ain't too far out of the way."

"I might grab a pizza anyway." She winked at him. "Don't tell Maggie."

He chuckled. "Well, okay."

Keisha followed his surprisingly fast pace through the residential streets, thinking of eating pizza in a warm bathtub. No one was in sight except for a group of kids playing in a huge hole at the side of the road. A smile tugged at her lips. She'd done the same thing as a child. If the road were a busy one, it might have been dangerous, but there wasn't much traffic in Forgotten.

She was so immersed in thought that she didn't really note her surroundings except they were heading northeast toward the turkey plant, Gobbler Farms. The closer they got to the plant, the fewer houses there were because of the smell on days when the wind blew just right—or wrong, as the residents there thought of it.

When the truck ahead stopped, her heart nearly did too. She knew this house. As a member of the Ladies Auxiliary in Forgotten, she had done rounds on the empty and abandoned houses, of which this was one.

It was where Xander Greenwood had lived.

CHAPTER 5

Even as Keisha stared up in dread, she saw a bucketful of water fly out the attic window onto the already soaked yard below, if the weedy, muddy mess could be called a yard. It was cut short enough, but weeds had decidedly taken over.

Ernie climbed out of his truck and began to remove the ladder from the back. Keisha was tempted to drive off. After all, Xander wouldn't let the old man climb the ladder in the rain, would he? But did Xander know anything about roofs? The man she'd known might have gone on to learn home repairs, but this man who conversed in medical terms was a complete stranger.

As she stared at the house, a small, pale face appeared in the window but disappeared almost instantly as Xander took its place. He shouted something to Ernie, which Keisha couldn't hear, before disappearing himself.

With a sinking heart, she climbed heavily from her car, slamming the door harder than necessary.

"Then get back inside," she muttered to herself as rain hit her face despite the hood. "He doesn't need two good Samaritans." Not when a hot bath and pizza called to her. Yet she felt obligated to both him and Ernie, as well as curious about the child. She wondered if the boy or girl looked like Xander or their mother. One thing for sure, their mother was as white as he was, which would make her full-blooded African American aunt happy that he had chosen his own kind.

The idea didn't make Keisha happy; it made her sad and angry. But wasn't this exactly what she needed? To see that there was nothing between them, and that he was happy. Because she couldn't reconcile the man who'd clung to her and begged her to return so they could elope with the man who had abandoned her when she needed him most.

Xander was at the front door by the time she reached it, once again wearing his blue jacket. His gaze fell over her, lingering in a way that made her blood pump faster. Good thing her skin was so dark, or he might be able to tell she was flushing.

"Keisha was kind enough to lend us her ladder," Ernie said.

"Oh, right." He tore his gaze from hers. Did he sound disappointed? "That's good because I can't bail out the water fast enough to leave it to find help. But I've rummaged through the shed and found some stuff that will work to hammer over it."

"Just be aware that you'll have to fix the nail holes later," Ernie said.

Xander chuckled. "I think the whole roof will probably need replacing."

"Well, tell me where it is, and I'll make a temporary fix." Ernie gazed up at the roof.

"No!" Keisha and Xander said together.

"I can do it," Xander added. "But I could use some help bailing in the attic, if you don't mind. Not sure how long fixing this will take, and the kids could barely keep it going when I went to the shed."

"Sure." Ernie set the ladder against the side of the house.

Kids? Keisha thought. Xander had certainly been busy.

Inside, the house was exactly as it had been when she last saw it when she'd checked on it as part of the Ladies Auxiliary. Besides an abandoned cardboard box and a large number of mismatched knickknacks pushed together on the coffee table—all powdered with a healthy layer of dust—the house could still have been occupied. The couches looked old but inviting, and the built-in shelves featured a small collection of old metal cars.

When Xander's mother left, either she hadn't wanted to be burdened by her parents' belongings, or she had forgotten them. The antiques shop in town would probably be interested in some of the contents. She opened her mouth to say so but decided it wasn't her place.

Everywhere she looked there were pieces of handcrafted wood. She hadn't known Xander's grandfather, but her parents' bookshelf in their home library looked much like the one in this living room. Or rather, it had before the fire.

Only when they reached the upstairs hallway did she see signs of the water. One end of the hallway carpet was soggy as they sloshed over it. She now wished she'd stopped to put on boots instead of her tennis shoes. Up in the attic, two little blond girls were awkwardly bailing water from a huge rain barrel that Keisha recognized as coming from Maggie's garage. Overhead, water poured down in a steady stream.

"This sucks!" said the girl with flyaway hair and wet jeans.

"Watch your language," Xander admonished.

"Yeah, or I'll tell Mom," said the other child with a smirk. "But

Xander, I'm cold," she added in a whine. And no wonder, since her pink princess dress was soaked down the entire front. At least her hair looked neat in the single braid.

Besides the obvious difference in clothing and hair, the girls appeared identical, and they looked an awful lot like Xander. Were they twins? Her heart gave a tug of remorse. She might have had a child by now, though never as pale as these two little beauties.

"Meet my little sisters, Sammy and Lila," Xander said, pointing at each girl respectively.

A brief panic swept through Keisha as she took it all in, trying to process. These little girls were Xander's sisters, and maybe they were one of the things she didn't remember after the accident. Like the classes she'd been taking and the paper she'd been writing. None of it had been familiar. Only Xander had stood out in her mind . . . and he never came to see her at the hospital.

"They thought they'd have fun hanging out with me today," Xander continued, "but we didn't count on this rain."

"I'll say," muttered Lila, plunging a large bowl into the barrel. "It would have been better staying home with Mom, even if she's sick."

Sammy blinked at her. "Are you kidding? This is cool! It's like we're on a boat, and we have to get the water out or die! And we get to explore this house . . . or we will if we can ever get the roof to stop leaking."

"A boat, huh?" Lila said thoughtfully as she tromped to the window with a little bit of water in the bowl. "Maybe."

Xander hurried after her. "Let me zip up your jacket. Do you want mine too? I don't need it."

Lila shook her head. "Yours is too big."

"Right." Xander bent to pick up a piece of wood and some

plastic near the window. Keisha bet he really had tried to get out on the roof from the window, and she was glad Ernie had stopped him.

Ernie picked up a bucket and began bailing water. "You gals fill up the containers, and I'll carry them to the window. But try to get a little more in when you do, okay? We don't want to be here all day. I got a free lunch and butter cake from Maggie waiting for me in the car."

"Maggie from the café?" Lila asked. "We had some too. It was so gooey and yummy!"

Now that Keisha thought about it, she recalled young girls coming into the café with Xander's mother a few times during the three years she worked there. She'd probably met them before, but it had been a very long time ago, and she didn't remember them or the fact that they were twins. She'd also seen his mother at the Walmart a time or two in Panna Creek, but she'd always been alone.

His hands full, Xander was struggling awkwardly to tuck a hammer under his arm, so Keisha took it from him. "I got it."

"Thanks." He said nothing further as he climbed down the ladder-like stairs with the board and plastic. Keisha followed. It wasn't as if she could let him go up on the roof all alone. He could slide off and die before Ernie knew what happened.

Outside, Xander moved the ladder around to the side of the house near the garage and adjusted the height. Tucking the hammer into his jeans, he started up. Keisha watched, her face battered by the rain, as he reached the top and stood, balancing as he stepped onto the roof and disappeared.

He came back within seconds. "I hate to ask, but I need to bring the ladder up here to reach the attic roof, so if you could maybe hold it there, that would help. It's not very steep here, so I don't think you'll fall. But I don't dare climb up to the next level without some support. If you'd rather not, I can go back to the shed to find wood to nail onto the roof as a base for the ladder."

She gave a slight snort. "You're going to trust me with your life?" He had nerve after what he'd done. If she gave the ladder a good push, it would be less than he deserved.

He studied her for several long seconds. "It's only my life, not my heart." His eyes held a deep sadness that sparked something in her that she never wanted to feel: hope.

No. He'd betrayed her and all their dreams and plans. This hope wasn't hers. She was simply affected by her uncle and the spark in his eyes.

"You think you can do it?" Xander asked when she didn't move or respond.

In answer, she started up the ladder. As promised, the roof wasn't too slick, but it was cold, and she wished she had put on something warmer. At least the jacket kept her sweater dry. They propped the ladder legs on either side of the garage apex, and she held it against the higher roof as he climbed. The best thing about these older houses was that the roofs weren't tall. Not like her aunt's house with its vaulted ceilings and pointed gables. Still, she should have told him that if he started to slide off, he should make sure not to land on his head.

Dumb. Dumb, she thought, glad she'd kept her mouth shut for once.

After a while, she heard pounding that seemed to go on far longer than her icy hands could endure. But at last, he reappeared, climbing down with a satisfied grin on his face.

"Looks like the plastic that was there came loose in the wind, and with the way it folded, it was catching all the rain and funneling it right down into the hole. I straightened the plastic and covered it with a layer of wood to keep everything in place. Hopefully, it'll last until I can get a roofer out here."

"Good." She started to pull the ladder extension down, but a sudden gust of wind caught her off balance. She stepped wide to counter the movement. Aat the same time, Xander reached for her and pulled her close.

"Whoa there," he said.

Her breath sucked between clenched teeth. How could it be that after all this time, she wanted only to fall into his arms and feel his heart beating against hers?

"I'm okay." She pushed away from him and almost fell for real. When her feet weren't scrambling anymore, she started back to the edge of the garage roof without looking at him, leaving him to deal with the ladder. She needed to get out of here. She needed to get her comfort food and soak in that warm bath.

Xander held the top of the ladder while she climbed down, and then she held the bottom while he descended. His grin sent a dart to her heart. "Guess we better go see if it worked, huh?"

No, I don't care. But she followed him back inside, where the girls had given up bailing to stare at the ceiling. The water only occasionally dripped now, probably more from residue than from new water entering the repair.

"You did it!" Lila said, running to her brother. "Now can we leave?"

"We haven't explored yet!" Sammy protested.

"But I'm cold."

"We can't stay here," Xander said. "Let's go to the Butter Cake and wrap you in blankets while your clothes dry."

"Maggie has a washer and dryer and extra clothes left behind from people who stayed there," Keisha couldn't help saying.

Sammy's shoulders slumped. "But the house. I'm sure Grandpa hid treasure."

"Maybe the rain will stop tomorrow," Xander said. "It's not like the house is going anywhere."

Ernie was still bailing. "We ought to at least pull back the carpet to start drying it. And this water level needs to be down enough in case the repair doesn't hold."

"Oh, it'll hold." Xander picked up a bowl. "But you're right. Give me ten more minutes, girls."

Keisha felt invisible. It was as if he'd written her out of his life again as easily as he had four and a half years ago. She edged toward the stairs and went down them without anyone noticing.

Once she hit the soggy carpet, she fled out to her car, where she tried to call for a pizza before realizing the cell tower must be out. She stopped on her way home to get pizza anyway.

Finally, in the hot bath, her skin warm and her stomach glutted with comforting cheese, she shut her eyes and sighed. But thoughts of Xander Greenwood were like salad oils that wouldn't wash easily off the plates at the café. She scrubbed her hair and skin vigorously, willing her mind to move on. Then her hand paused as it always did on the ugly scar slashing across the front of her right leg, and her mind did move on, though not in a good direction. Her fingers traced the uneven path the scar made from her right hip down to the spot where the tips of her fingers could reach without bending her waist. The thickened flesh was an inch wide in some places, and in one section, several scars collided, making a crisscrossing, bumpy washboard. The skin was no longer an angry red, but the ugly, white, stretched skin made her feel like a monster, exactly as it had when she'd first seen it all stitched up like a limb belonging to Frankenstein.

After the accident, the pain had been so great that the scar hadn't mattered as much. Now, it was a constant reminder of how much she'd lost. Every day she rubbed in vitamin E in an effort to lessen the marks and ease the tightness of the scar tissue, but after the first year, it never changed. So she stuck to wearing longer skirts and shorts and tried to forget.

Doc once told her that additional surgery might help remove parts of the scar, but he didn't recommend the risk of a cosmetic fix. He simply couldn't understand how the scar was a lasting reminder of how she'd lost everything.

No, not everything, though it had seemed that way at the time. Seeing Xander again made all the old feelings rise inside her. Feelings of both abandonment and love.

And there she was thinking of Xander again. Why, oh why had he come back to town? Maybe she would have to leave herself, or at least hide until the snake returned to whatever hole he had crawled out of.

Yes, that was it. It wasn't as if he'd be around long.

Feeling slightly better, she drained the water and was in her robe putting away the leftover pizza when the doorbell rang. Her heart jumped happily.

"No," she groaned. She would ignore it. She'd go upstairs to cuddle with Cupcake and watch something with a lot of action and killing—nothing romantic or heartbreaking. Then tomorrow she'd return to work, and if Xander happened to be there, well, she'd face him down.

The doorbell rang again. And again.

No doubt about who it was after that, and if she didn't answer, she'd pay a steep price.

Sighing, she hurried to the front door and opened it. Sure enough, there stood a striking, ebony-skinned woman in dress pants and high heels, a tan, folded umbrella in her hand. Olivia

Campbell, her aunt. As usual, her face was expertly made up, and the long, iron-straight, black hair—a particularly expensive wig—was perfectly in place.

Keisha forced a smile. "Hi, Olivia."

Olivia's eyes ran down Keisha's purple robe that had decidedly seen better days. "Why are you in your robe at *this* time of day? And answering the door?"

"You rang three times," Keisha pointed out.

"Well, I knew you were here. Your car wasn't at the café, and it is here. Now are you going to invite me in or not?"

Keisha looked past her at the street where her gray BMW was parked. Rain was still coming down in torrents. "Yeah, sure, but I thought you didn't drive in the rain." She stepped back so Olivia could come in.

"I drive when I need to as long as it isn't far," she said with the faintest offended sniff. "Is that pizza?"

Keisha didn't know if her offense was because of her comment about the rain or the pizza aroma permeating the house. "Yeah, it is."

Olivia's head swung back and forth. "You know what white flour does to a woman's figure."

"Hopefully, it'll make me gain a few pounds," Keisha responded with a lightheartedness she didn't feel. "With how I run around at the café, I need the calories."

"Well, the café is something else we should talk about."

Groaning internally, Keisha took Olivia's umbrella, leaned it against the wall on the small square of entry tile, and led her aunt further into the room that held a loveseat, end table, chair, and coffee table. The items were castoffs from Olivia's house, so she was bound to approve. Keisha sat on the loveseat, stifling the urge to pull her foot up under her. That wasn't kosher in Olivia's book unless you were in your personal sitting room with no visitors in sight. Keisha wished Cupcake had followed her into the room, so she had something to do with her hands, but like most of Forgotten, Cupcake didn't like Olivia, and the feeling was mutual.

An awkward silence fell between them, but Keisha was too mentally exhausted to make small talk. Olivia folded her hands in her lap. "I heard about the accident. I do hope it wasn't too stressful for you."

"I'm fine," Keisha said, but something tightened in her chest.

"I also heard about Xander Greenwood being back in town." Olivia's dark eyes pinned her to the love seat.

Ah, now Keisha understood the reason for the visit. Olivia usually demanded Keisha's presence at her house for weekly family dinners, where she liked to nitpick on Keisha for still working at the café instead of finishing her college degree. That, or talk about how burdensome it was to live in such a small town. She had never forgiven Keisha's father, her half-brother, for enticing her to Forgotten, or by extension, forgiven Keisha either.

"Is he?" Keisha feigned innocence. That was the best attack with Olivia, though she understood it was a lie of omission, which would have made her father shake his head. This was how it always went with Olivia—Keisha doing things she ordinarily wouldn't do to keep distance between them so Olivia wouldn't try to run her life. Why couldn't she stand up to the woman and tell her to mind her own business?

"Yes, and I want your promise that you will not get mixed up with him again."

"Oh, that's easy. I don't want anything to do with him."

"Good." Olivia leaned forward as if searching her eyes for

deceit. "I mean, he might be a doctor now, but it doesn't change where he came from. You are better than that."

The comment rankled. "By everything I've heard, his grandfather was a good man, and his mom was a hard worker."

Olivia looked disappointed. "You know what I mean. We need to stick with our own."

"Rich and black, you mean." The words left her mouth before she could stop them. Maybe it was the prestige of her uncle or her father, the attorney, but here in Forgotten, race had never been an issue for her, even if she'd been the only "black girl" in the high school. Of course, she'd run with the rich, popular crowd, if there was such a thing in Forgotten. Unlike Xander, who'd been born not only on the wrong side of the economic scale but also out of wedlock, which was notable, even in a town as forgiving as Forgotten.

"It's not that simple," Olivia said. "I promised your father I'd look after you, and that's what I'm doing." She brought a hand to the corner of her eye as if to blot a tear.

Keisha's heart ached with the old memories. She remembered all too well how Olivia had "protected" her. By decree of her father's will, Keisha would not come into her inheritance until age thirty unless she married before then. But the inheritance would only be hers upon marriage if Olivia approved of her future husband. Otherwise, she'd still have to wait until thirty to access her funds.

Olivia had never approved of Xander. In fact, when Keisha came home for spring break to announce that she and Xander were getting married and going to Africa for several years to build communities for people in need, Olivia had only laughed. "Then you'll be doing it without your inheritance," she'd said, her lip curling with a touch of ugliness.

"We don't care. Xander found us some sponsors. We don't have to pay."

"Maybe not now, but you'll see. He only wants your money. That's the kind of people they are. White trash."

"What on earth are you talking about?" Keisha had retorted. Even now, four years later, the exact words stood out in her mind. "He's worked his way through four years of college without help—or will in another month." Because their plans involved finishing out the school year. They weren't irresponsible. And so what if she had another year to go? Wherever she ended up working, a year or two of service would only look better on her resume.

"If you do this, you will always regret it." Olivia's words hung like a promise between them. "Mark my words."

But Keisha had known that the only thing she'd regret was not being with Xander. "He doesn't even know about the money," she'd protested. "He loves me, and I love him. We share the same dreams. Can't you see that's what matters?"

"It's not what your father wanted for you," Olivia had insisted. "If you do this, you do it alone."

Keisha had whirled from her that night and plunged into the rain, leaving the door to her aunt's house open. For once in her life, she was going to do what her heart demanded and go back to St. Louis where Xander waited. Her parents would understand.

She'd driven all the way to Kansas City before the accident occurred—the horrible accident that she barely survived. She remembered nothing of that first week and little of the second. But one thing she knew for sure: Xander never came for her.

Now she pushed the dark memories back into the deep hole where she normally kept them. That was the past, and even if, by some strange twist of events, Olivia welcomed Xander with open arms, Keisha wouldn't do the same. He had killed whatever they had, and though her body and heart remembered him, the new, stronger her was in charge now. Her aunt had been right, and Keisha would not fall into another trap.

"You don't need to worry about me," Keisha said now. "But I am worried about you and Josiah. I heard you're separating?" There, that would definitely change the subject.

Olivia's mouth tightened. "He shouldn't have told you."

"He didn't, not really. I figured it out."

Olivia lifted her chin. "I suppose the whole town will be talking about it soon, but I've reconnected with someone online that I might want to pursue a relationship with, and it's time to think about the future. I'll be here until Charlie graduates, of course, and then I'll be leaving Forgotten. It's only a few more years. Before I leave, I'd like to see you settled in a law school far away from here. With the funds your father marked for your education, you wouldn't even have to work. You have to see that the Butter Cake isn't your future."

Of course Olivia wanted her far away from this town. Her aunt had never belonged, though that was her own doing, not the town's. Keisha herself loved Forgotten fiercely enough to fight to belong. She hadn't always felt that way, but she did now.

"You know how I've always regretted cutting short my graduate education to stay here when I married Josiah," Olivia continued. "I don't want you to have the same regret."

Keisha already had regrets, plenty of them, though she wouldn't tell that to Olivia. But whatever else Olivia might be, she was right at least about her work at the café. "I'm ready to make some changes, and I do plan to finish my degree. As for the rest, I'll let you know when I figure it out." Keisha stood, hoping Olivia wouldn't push because there was nothing more to say. The only thing Keisha knew for certain was that the dream of being an attorney like her dad had died in the accident, along with almost every other part of her.

"Good." Olivia stood, nodding as if she'd won a battle. "I'd like you to come to dinner on Sunday. It'll just be Charlie and me."

"Okay. Sure." Keisha would go for Charlie, if for no other reason. He'd be hurting with his dad gone.

Keisha walked Olivia to the door, where she bent to retrieve Olivia's umbrella. "Thanks for stopping by." The words felt like another lie.

"Oh, and one more thing," Olivia said as Keisha opened the door. "I know you haven't really wanted to be involved in the investment portion of the money your dad left us, but I've bought half a dozen pieces of real estate here in town. With the pasta factory going in and possibly other larger businesses coming in as well, we'll be able to turn a nice profit in only a few years. That'll give you even more of a start when you finish law school or get married."

"That's smart. Thank you," Keisha said. If there was something Olivia was good at besides keeping house and dressing well, it was investing. She sent regular updates to Keisha and her accountant, and the numbers always went up. Her father had done that part right, at least, in trusting his sister.

Actually, Olivia had been right about Xander too. The thought made Keisha weary.

"Well, goodbye, dear."

Olivia had stepped out onto the tiny porch and opened her umbrella when something occurred to Keisha. "Olivia?" she said.

Her aunt turned to face her. "Yes?"

"How do you know Xander's a doctor?" Keisha didn't know that for sure herself. Back in college, he'd taken several medical classes, but as far as she was aware, he hadn't been planning on medical school.

Olivia stood very still as if the question surprised her. "Does it matter?"

"I'm just wondering." But suddenly it did matter—a lot.

Olivia pursed her lips slightly and then said, "Because when you were in the hospital, I gave him the deposit for his medical school on the condition that he left you alone."

Keisha's breath left her body in a sudden, violent rush. She stared, shocked, not knowing what to say. "H-he came to see you?"

Olivia nodded. "Yes. And I gave him three thousand dollars. That's what you were worth to him. Now you see why I don't want him anywhere near you." With that, she turned and marched back to her car, her spine rigid and her head lifted proudly.

Keisha stared after her, questions begging to burst from her throat, but she had no breath to voice them. She could barely breathe.

Overhead, the sky continued to cry.

Just like her heart.

CHAPTER 6

When Xander looked around on his next trip to empty his bucket of water, he noticed Keisha was gone. For an instant, he stood paralyzed, as if thrown back in time to the night when she hadn't returned to St. Louis, where he'd waited to begin his new life with her.

He dropped the bucket and hurried down the stairs and out to the front, but all he saw was her little red car in the distance. The old, familiar pain bit into his heart, making his breath stick in his throat.

He would do well to remember she wasn't his girlfriend anymore, that she'd wanted him gone so much she dumped him at first opportunity. She hadn't even faced him for the breakup but instead allowed her aunt to do her dirty work as if he wasn't worth her time. He'd certainly felt dirty and unworthy after talking to Olivia Campbell, like a gutter urchin she deigned to address. When he'd arrived on her doorstep looking for Keisha, she had acted amused at his insistence that he was going to marry her niece. Then, adding insult, she offered money for his loss as if it could make up for Keisha's rejection.

At first, he refused to believe that Keisha wasn't coming back—he had faith in their relationship. But as the days and weeks passed, and she hadn't reached out, he understood that Olivia had told him the truth about Keisha's feelings. Ultimately, he had Olivia to thank for becoming a doctor, and it had been the right thing for him in the end.

So why would he give it all up now to be in Africa with Keisha?

He became aware of the rain dripping down the back of his neck inside his clothes and realized he was standing in the yard—in a mud puddle, to be exact. His grandfather would be turning over in his grave, as the saying went, if he knew the condition of his house and yard.

Xander took a deep breath, breathing in the intoxicating scent of rain, pavement, and growing things. The farmers who hadn't finished harvesting would be delayed now, but most would likely be finished or not yet ready for the final harvest anyway. Farmers seemed to have a second sense about these things.

Shoulders slumping slightly, he went back inside to see the girls coming down the attic stairs with Ernie. "It'll keep now for a couple of days, I think," Ernie said. "But I'll leave the ladder just in case. I won't need it until it dries out a bit."

"Thank you for coming."

"What are neighbors for?"

That made Xander smile. "We're not exactly neighbors." Ernie lived in the lot next to the burned-out one where Keisha's parents' house had stood. Rumor had it he'd been the one to call the fire department that night. When Xander had known Keisha, she still felt guilt over not being there when the electrical fire started, but she'd mostly come to terms with it. According to Keisha, her parents had been deeply attached to one another, and going together prevented a lot of mourning.

"It would have killed them to be apart," she'd said. "And I know they wouldn't want me moping around. So I've tried not to."

Xander had kissed her soundly under the tree outside the library. "That's how I feel. As long as we're together, it doesn't matter where we are."

"I love you too," she said, kissing him back.

His thoughts of the past scattered as Ernie harrumphed like the old man he was. "Nonsense. We're all neighbors in Forgotten. I drive by this house every time I pick up my turkey order. You get a fifteen percent discount if you order directly, you know."

"I'll keep that in mind."

"Besides, your grandpa and I were great friends. You know we were in high school together, don't you?"

Xander wanted to say yes, but the truth was he couldn't remember who Ernie was in the stories of his grandfather's life—stories that were as vivid as a movie to him even now: his grandpa raising his first goat for the county fair, beating out the jocks in the high school footrace, helping his father build this house, serving a stint in the Navy, and marrying his grandmother. Jim Greenwood had been a storyteller for sure, especially when talking about his volunteer service in Africa, and his vivid stories of that time had ignited something in Xander that had never died. His grandfather was the best man he'd ever known, and Xander knew he was lucky to have had him in his life. Though his death had been hard, his grandfather's gifts stayed with him, as did the determination to make himself into someone his grandfather would admire.

"The time Jim beat out all the jocks in that footrace is still a matter of discussion when we old farts gather at the Butter Cake," Ernie said with a sigh. "That was a good day for all of us."

Sammy giggled at Ernie's word choice while Lila tugged on Xander's hand. "He said a bad word."

"It's only bad if you're a little girl," Ernie said, grinning at her.

Lila moved behind Xander to hide from Ernie as Sammy said, "I fart all the time, and I'm a girl. And when I grow up, I'm going to marry Jacob Wright because he thinks girls are just as good at climbing trees as boys."

"Oh yeah?" Ernie nodded sagely. "Well, I suppose that's as good a reason as any. Probably would have a lot fewer divorces these days if that was our only expectation."

Sammy stared hard at him for a few seconds but apparently decided he wasn't mocking her. She smiled. "Well, let's get to exploring."

"Nope," Xander said. "We're going back to the Butter Cake. You both need a hot bath and dry clothes."

Ernie grinned his approval. "Good idea. With all the humidity in the air, pulling up the carpet can wait for a day or two when the heat comes back. But no more than that, mind you. Don't want the house smelling like mold if you're going to live here." His eyes narrowed. "Or are you here to sell?"

"I don't know, actually. I'm just here at the moment to make sure the taxes are all paid up and that there aren't any pressing repairs, which it appears there are."

Ernie chuckled. "Yeah, but the bones of this house are strong. Did your grandpa tell you we helped build this house?" At Xander's nod, he added, "Yep. Mostly screws, not nails, and double the nails when we did use them. Built to last."

Xander experienced a rush of pride that he'd never felt in relation to this house. With its location so close to the turkey farm, he'd been more embarrassed than anything in his youth. Maybe he should think about moving here instead of renting that apartment in Panna Creek. It would add twenty minutes or more to his daily commute, but it would save money in the long run.

Except Keisha was here, and the vision of her car driving away still burned in his mind. Would this town be large enough to hold both of them and all their unfinished business? Because he knew she felt it too.

Probably just guilt, he thought. Would it even make a difference to her or her aunt now that he'd become a doctor? He doubted it, and if it did, well, that wasn't exactly a good thing. It had been one of the reasons he hadn't told her about his acceptance to medical school in Washington DC when their paths first crossed in college. He'd wanted to be sure that wasn't what drew her to him. And he hadn't told her later because he'd been plagued with second, third, and fourth thoughts about his career choice. Med school meant more years of education, thousands of dollars of debt, and no chance to follow in his grandfather's footsteps to do something wild and free in his youth, something that mattered on a basic, day-to-day level. Building a community that would save lives while making a permanent difference for the most vulnerable and needy had seemed to be a way to do that, and Keisha had agreed.

Or so he'd thought. Maybe she'd decided to send a check instead. Yet that didn't explain what she was still doing in Forgotten or why when she looked at him, he felt the need to beg for forgiveness.

"Come on, girls," he said, becoming aware of Ernie and Lila staring at him. Sammy, of course, was nowhere to be seen. He raised his voice. "Sammy, I'm leaving. Come now, or I won't let you explore tomorrow!"

That was assuming his mother would let him keep the girls here until tomorrow afternoon. He'd call from the Butter Cake to make sure unless the landlines were also down.

He held out a hand to Ernie. "Thanks again, Mr. Pike. I really appreciate it."

"Give me a call, and I'll help you with the carpet. Maggie has my number. I do all her plumbing when she can't figure it out herself." Ernie chuckled. "Or when that new husband of hers can't figure it out. Plumbing ain't as easy as flying a plane, apparently." Still chuckling, he shuffled out the door, the graying hair on his head so thin in the back that the pink of his scalp shone through.

From the door, Xander and Lila watched him shuffle to his truck and drive away.

"Nice guy," Xander said.

"He said fart," Lila murmured in disapproval.

"I think he's cool." Sammy appeared from nowhere with a small, wooden chest in her hands. "At least for an old guy."

"Let's get out to the truck." Xander shooed them out, feeling suddenly weary.

"Can I take this box?"

Xander peered at it. It was made of a dark wood, perhaps cherry, and the carvings seemed less skilled than his grandfather's. "Sure, but don't lose anything that might be inside. Could be important."

Sammy stared at him with a doubtful twist to her lips. "Probably not, or mom wouldn't have left it here. We can put treasure in it when we find some."

"Right. Okay then. Everyone have their jackets? Let's go."

Xander was hungry after all the activity, but once up in their room at the Butter Cake, he bathed the girls in the adjoining bathroom before tucking them into the queen-sized canopy bed and turning on the television. Both wore adult T-shirts that went to their knees, courtesy of Maggie. He'd borrowed one also, along with a pair of her husband's sweatpants.

"You stay right here, and I'll get us some lunch," he told the girls.

"Okay," they chimed, not taking their stares away from the television.

He paused at the corner table where Sammy had placed the small carved chest. Deep layers of dust covered the surface, so ingrained with humidity that most of it stayed in place when he rubbed his finger over it. He lifted the lid to see the documents that hadn't been of any interest to Sammy. The first was a list of supplies and quantities related to building. Under that was an old school certificate for woods shop. Was there also one for winning the footrace? Xander hoped so, but a quick glance through showed newspaper clippings about people whose names he vaguely recognized, a few letters, and random papers that had no meaning to him. Maybe his mother would want the clippings.

Shutting the lid, he strode to the door and paused. "And I really do mean stay here," he emphasized.

"Can we have butter cake if we do?" Sammy asked.

"The two aren't connected. I may or may not get you cake. But either way, you will stay put." He gave them his most confident doctor stare, the one he'd practiced in med school.

Sammy squirmed. "Okay, okay." Her eyes drifted back to the television.

Satisfied, Xander hurried down the stairs, where he transferred the girls' clothing from the washer to the dryer. The landline on the wall reminded him that he hadn't called his mother. Had there been one upstairs in his room? Probably.

He found the number on his phone and dialed. "Hey, it's me," he said.

"Are you on your way back?" His mother sounded distant and sleepy against a background of noise. So much for hoping she'd been resting this morning. Who could sleep with all that din?

"Not exactly. It's been raining like crazy here. Isn't it raining there?"

"Just a minute." The background noise cut out, and for a moment, he could only hear a bare hint of breathing. "Oh, yes," she said. "It's raining here too. Wow, it's coming down strong."

"I was worried the road would flood."

"I'm sure it has. Every year there's talk here and in Forgotten about raising that part of the road and putting in a drain, but they never do it."

"I think we'll stay at the Butter Cake tonight, if that's okay. Maggie lent the girls T-shirts they can sleep in, and she has toothbrushes."

His mother laughed. "I'm sure the girls are in heaven, but they might be driving you crazy."

"Not too bad. I'll have them back soon after the rain stops. They wanted to explore the house a bit tomorrow, though, before we head your way. Is that okay?"

"Sure. There's nothing there that can hurt them. I bet it's a dusty mess."

"Some, yes, and we've got a roof leak. We'll have to fix it if you want to sell."

"Me?" She sounded surprised. "I don't want anything to do with the house. It's yours, Xander. Grandpa wanted you to have it. When I asked you to look into it, I meant that it's yours. You'll probably have to pay back taxes, but you can do whatever you want—sell it, fix it up, live in it." She sounded hopeful at the end of this. "I hear the smell isn't so bad in the summers anymore since Gobbler Farms started selling turkey manure fertilizer. They had to conform to some guidelines. But I don't know the details."

Xander couldn't help smiling. "Too bad they didn't do that in the old days."

She laughed. "Even with the smell, we did all right."

"Anyway, I'm sorry about not getting them home."

"It's okay. I trust you. You're their brother, and who better than a doctor to keep an eye on them?"

"Speaking of that, did you take your medicine? And keep to your diet?"

She gave a little groan. "Yes, like I have all week, and I do feel better. It's just not much fun."

"It'll come easier once you're stable. All those ups and downs are hard on you." And dangerous, but he didn't add the words. He'd already pressed that subject with her, and he didn't want more tears.

"I know. Well, say hi to Maggie for me. I'd ask you to bring me butter cake, but I know your answer."

"You can have a little with a meal, Mom."

More laughter. "I'm just teasing."

For a moment, there was only silence, and then he asked, "So, are there any rumors or news I should know about Forgotten?" His heart gave a painful thump. Why was he doing this to himself? It wasn't as if she'd been following Keisha's activities. Back in college, he mentioned they were dating, but he had been waiting until he and Keisha eloped to tell her how serious it was.

He hadn't wanted her to make a fuss and insist on throwing a party, not with new twin babies needing all her attention while her husband was on the road. They'd planned to visit her before their flight to Africa. A flight that, in the end, they never scheduled.

"As far as I know, only the pasta factory is new, and a few dozen houses. Rumor is that land values will go up, so it's a good time to take care of the house. Oh, and Maggie got married. I wasn't there, but everyone I ran into mentioned it. Speaking of Maggie, is that pretty girl you used to date still working at the Butter Cake? It's been a year or more since I saw her there."

His heart decided that was its cue to speed up. "Do you mean Keisha?"

"Yes, that lovely mulatto girl. She's as beautiful as her parents were. May God rest their souls."

"She's still here." He was still puzzled about why Keisha was working at the café instead of practicing law, but the subject hadn't come up between them. "Well, I'd better go. I'm getting the girls a late lunch and hoping they'll be happy with what's on TV. Because otherwise, I'm in for a long night."

Her laughter came over the line. "Better you than me."

"Right. Take care of yourself. And call me here if you can't get me on my cell. The storm must have knocked out a tower."

"Will do. And thanks, Xander. I'm so happy you came here to do your residency. I've missed you so much."

"I'm glad too." Truthfully, he hadn't missed his mother while he'd been away and busy, but now that he was back, he felt the bond of mother and son pulling him into its safe confines, filled with both duty and love. "I love you," he added.

"I love you too, son."

He hung up and hurried out of the laundry room and around

the corner toward the direction of the counter, almost running into Maggie.

"Oh," she said with a laugh, flushing a little. "Sorry about that. I was going to check on the girls' clothes."

"I switched them to the dryer. Thanks so much."

Maggie blinked. "Good. Except you shouldn't dry Lila's costume. It could possibly shrink. It will hang dry just fine by morning."

He sprinted back and rescued the dress, which thankfully looked no worse off. Disaster averted, he returned to the counter. Only three groups of people were in the café, mostly construction workers he assumed were waiting out the rain in order to return to work on the new pasta factory.

"What do you have for kids?" he asked Maggie. "Something they'll eat."

Maggie grinned. "I know just the thing. Cheese fingers, which is really an open-faced grilled cheese sandwich cut in fours, served with a side of sliced apples and baby carrots with Ranch dressing. Your choice of juice."

"Sounds perfect. They aren't that picky, but they are kids. My mom's been sick, and she has a hard time getting them to eat healthy. I don't want that to affect them when they're older."

"I'm sorry to hear about Allison. I hope she'll be okay."

"Her diabetes went untreated for too long. She was probably borderline for years. We just need to get her stable and into some new habits. She's on insulin now, which is helping."

"Type 1 then?" Maggie said.

"Yes."

"Well, she might be sick, but the few times I've seen her, she looked happy."

Xander smiled. "I think she is. I mean, her husband is away

more than they both like with the truck driving, but they make it work."

"I'm glad you're here to help out, and I'm sure you've made her proud. Go ahead and have a seat. I won't be long fixing your plates."

"I'd better go check on the girls. One time during medical school, I was late checking on some little patients, and they somehow wandered into the nurses' breakroom."

Maggie laughed. "There's nothing they can get into or hurt here. But why don't I bring your meals upstairs for you? We aren't busy today. What would you like?"

The moment she mentioned food, his hunger came roaring back. "Maybe surprise me. After working my way through college and going to med school, I eat anything but liver, snails, frog legs, and avocados."

She laughed again. "Right. Well, of those we only have avocado, so that's easy enough to avoid."

"Oh, and where should I go to find out about back taxes for my mother's—my—house?" he asked.

"That's wise because if the taxes go unpaid for too long, the city auctions off the houses."

"Then I need to take care of that while I decide what to do about the rooftop. The hole is pretty bad."

"A shingle or three must have fallen off, and the wood underneath rotted," Maggie said.

"That's what it looks like to me."

"Well, if that's all you have to fix, it'll be lucky."

"And the carpet."

A grin spread across her face. "Long overdue."

He laughed. "Probably." It was easy talking with Maggie. Like it had once been with Keisha.

"As for your question, just call city hall and ask for Penny Jenkins. She can look it up or point you to the records clerk. We do have one, but Penny can access anything. She keeps the little things running smoothly so the mayor can do his job."

The mayor, meaning Keisha's uncle, Josiah Campbell, had been Forgotten's mayor since Xander was in high school. Xander had always admired the man, but maybe his congeniality was only a part of his public persona. He'd probably sided with his wife, Olivia, when Keisha left Xander.

"You can use the phone upstairs in the room," Maggie said. "I have a binder there with all the town highlights and important numbers. I'll be up in a few." She turned gracefully and disappeared into her kitchen.

Xander stared after her, a question about Keisha dying on his tongue. Which was for the best, he decided. However, that didn't stop his brain. He kept going through their meetings today, especially that moment on the roof when it was all he could do not to wrap his arms around her and bury his face in her neck to breathe in her sweet scent. He missed that more than anything—the feel and smell of her. He'd had to force himself to let go because if he held on a moment longer, he would have been lost.

Shaking the thoughts away didn't work, so he replaced them with the image of her driving away. She wasn't reliable, and he hadn't spent the last four years building his life just to let her wreck it again. If he hadn't gone to medical school, he might not have been able to dig himself out of depression. Fortunately, the letter reminding him about his student deposit arrived soon after she was gone, and that letter, in a very real way, saved him and gave him focus.

Upstairs, the girls were still glued to the television, so he took the portable landline into the bathroom and closed the door.

His cell phone might not be working, but at least the electricity hadn't gone off, or both the television and this phone would be useless, and the television was all that was saving him with the girls right now. The more time he spent with them, the more he realized he didn't know about kids. Strange to think if he and Keisha had married, they might have one of their own by now.

Stop, he told himself. A child would have been impossible in med school, and school was the one thing that had gone right in his life. In a few years, he'd be making good money, and then it would be time to settle down.

He dialed city hall before his traitorous brain could send him more images of Keisha and the child they never had.

"Hi," he said when they answered. "Can I talk to Penny Jenkins? Thanks."

A kind-sounding woman came on the line almost instantly, and he told her who he was and explained about the house. "The thing is, my mother wants me to have the house, and I don't know anything about where it stands with back taxes, but my mother mentioned a notice or two. She lives in Panna Creek, and she's been dealing with twins and diabetes."

"Poor Allison. That's a lot on her plate. I wish she would have told me the last time I saw her at Walmart. I would have made sure she got the notices. Anyway, it's good she has you."

"Well, I hope to help. Besides, she wants me to have the house, so we need to know how to transfer it to my name. I'm assuming it's in hers now, though it could still be in my grandfather's."

"I'll check on that too. Normally, I'd send you to records, but our clerk's wife called about some flooding at their house, and he had to run home." She paused for a moment. "Hmm, let me bring up the files. Can you give me the address? That will help when we don't know who the listed owner is."

Xander told her and then peeked out the door at the kids. Their mouths were open and their eyes glazed as they stared at the television. Maybe it would have been better if he let them explore the old house instead of feeding their media addiction.

"Okay," Penny said in his ear. "I found it. Unfortunately, I have bad news. It went up for auction last week because the taxes haven't been paid in over ten years. To give you a reference, after three unpaid years, it can go up for auction. The house and all the contents have been sold."

The idea of someone else owning his grandfather's house made Xander feel sick, although before today, he hadn't thought of the house at all. "But it's still just sitting there," he protested. "The rain nearly filled up the whole attic today. I had to climb up on the roof to get it stopped, and that was only a temporary fix."

"Well, it's hard to find construction workers out here, especially with the pasta factory going in. Most of those guys are brought in by the company, but they hired a lot of locals too. That means there's probably a waitlist for work you want done."

"But I didn't even know about the taxes," he said, frustration creeping into his tone. "At least not until two weeks ago. Isn't there anything I can do about the sale?" And when she meant everything in the house belonged to someone else now, did that mean his cars too? He fisted his free hand, trying to control his emotions.

"There is something you can do," Penny said. "But first let me explain. Your house had back taxes, fees, and interest of nearly eight thousand dollars, but it sold at auction for twenty-eight thousand, which means as the current listed owner, your mother has the right to claim the overages or the difference."

"You mean, it's like we sold the house . . . in a bargain-basement fire sale."

"Yeah, just about. But the buyer understands there's a redemption period in which the original owners can pay the back taxes and fees. In that case, we would return the buyer's money and cancel their deed from the sale. That redemption period might be another reason why no work has been done. Though, generally, something like a leak is a priority and would have been considered reimbursable if the heirs decided to redeem."

"Okay, then how long do we have to redeem the house?" Not that he wanted to, but he needed to know.

"Well, it's considered an abandoned building and not a homestead since no one has been living there and it's not a primary residence, but even so, our state law says owners or heirs have up to a year to redeem it. As I mentioned, that means your mother will have to immediately pay the city any delinquent taxes and fees associated with the property, plus anything the new owner might have spent on necessary upkeep. Or she can transfer the right of redemption to you, and you can do all that."

Xander sighed. "How much of the back taxes were fees?"

"A lot," she admitted. "About triple is what I see here."

"So because we didn't pay a few thousand over ten years, we have to pay eight thousand now?" For a house in a small town where property taxes were low, the number was astronomical, especially for a house they supposedly already owned. He estimated the money would have gone a long way toward repairing the roof and perhaps even covered it entirely.

"Yeah, it really stinks." She hesitated. "Your grandpa was loved around here, though, so you might get a discount on past taxes if you can get the city council to sign off on it. In fact, you can turn in a petition to the town council right away. They're meeting here tomorrow like they do every Thursday morning. I'm sure many people would be happy to have the Greenwoods back in town, especially after what you did for Laina this morning."

Apparently, he was the talk of the town's rumor mill.

"Poor Keisha," Penny added. "How ironic for her to be first on the scene. Must have been super hard on her after all she's been through."

He supposed she was talking about the death of Keisha's parents, but before he could decide if he should press for more information—the woman seemed willing to talk—he heard a commotion in the other room.

"Oh, looks like I have to go," he said. "I have my little twin sisters with me, and something's going on."

Penny laughed. "Better hurry. You have time with this redemption thing, but I'd take care of it sooner rather than later—before the buyer puts money into the house."

"I will." He'd have to weigh the options. He was earning money now as a resident, but it wasn't yet the big bucks they all dreamed about in med school, and his school loan payments were more than he cared to think about. He could potentially defer them this year, but if he didn't redeem the house, his mother could keep the overage money, and he knew she could use the funds right now. But not redeeming didn't make any long-term sense, even if he didn't stay in town, because he would be able to fix up the house and sell it for a lot more than the overages, even after paying the taxes and repairs. If he could find the time, that is. That would be an issue with his new schedule.

"Hey," he said, "if we decide not to redeem, can I at least take some of my things from the house?" He wished he hadn't left his grandfather's cars there now.

"That would be up to the new owner because it was sold as-is. They might be happy if you cleaned out some, or they might want to sell you the items, especially if they're valuable vintage pieces."

Xander groaned internally. With his luck, the person who bought his house was a money-grubbing monster. "Well, so who won the auction for my house? Is it someone local? Or an out-of-town investor?" Local would be better because even if they didn't know him, they might know his family. Forgotten had only three thousand, seven hundred and eighty-six people, according to the sign he'd seen coming into town, and while he didn't know all of them, he knew plenty or had heard of them.

"Well, uh . . ." Reluctance entered her tone. "Of course I can tell you. It's a matter of public record, but keep in mind that you'd go through us if you redeem the house, not through the buyer."

"Right. But they'd have to give me permission to take my grandfather's furniture or any of my childhood toys?"

"Sounds rotten, doesn't it?"

"I guess we should have cleaned them out before now." It was partly his fault, even if he didn't want to admit it.

"Well, life gets in the way sometimes. Anyway, the buyer on record is Keisha Jefferson."

CHAPTER 7

Keisha was getting ready for work and listening to the rain hitting against the windows when her cell phone rang, making her jump after a night of no service and old DVDs instead of online streaming. She glanced at the caller ID before picking up.

"Hey, Charlie, what's up?" She wondered if her aunt and uncle had told him about the divorce or if she should be careful about what she said. Surely he had to notice his father was no longer sleeping at the house.

"I'm calling to see if you can give me a ride to the vet clinic."

"Where are you? Aren't you in school?" She looked in the mirror and gave her hair one last brush. It looked much better than yesterday, more curl than frizz now, but the ends were still straight from the chemicals. If she hadn't been going to put her hair up for work, she'd curl the ends to help them blend in. Only because she wanted to look nice and *not* because she might run into Xander at the café.

"I'm at home. Mom usually takes me to school, but they canceled it because there's some kind of sinkhole outside the school, and they're worried people are going to drive into it and fall to China or something. That's where Mom is right now, doing something with the city council to see if they can get it fixed before Monday." He gave a soft snort. "They won't be able to if it don't stop raining."

Keisha refrained from correcting his grammar, knowing he got enough of that from his mom.

"Besides, she wouldn't want to take me to the clinic anyway. She thinks being a vet is for people who can't hack being a doctor. Dad's the one who always drives me there, and he's already at work. In a meeting, actually. Do you have time to come and get me before you go to the café?"

Keisha pulled back her phone and glanced at the time. "Yes, I can. I just have to finish getting ready for work and feed Cupcake."

"How is she doing? Did her paw heal okay?" He'd removed part of a puncture vine from it last week at family dinner.

"She's perfect, thanks to you. But I'd better hurry and get ready now. I'll see you in a few."

"Thanks. You're the best."

She smiled, knowing her cousin really did think so. She'd been ten when he was born, and he had followed her around since he could walk. They were the only kids in both their families, and he was more like a brother than a cousin, especially after her parents died, and she began spending college holidays and summer vacations with his family.

Keisha decided on an easy but fancy-looking twist for her hair instead of her normal ponytail. And this time she'd be sure to take an umbrella. Her aunt and uncle's house was near Forgotten

Reservoir, and it was easily the biggest house in the area. Sadly, Olivia had cleared a lot of the old trees on the property for the huge expanse of lawn in front, but Keisha had to admit that the grass and trees on the side framed the house perfectly.

Charlie was waiting for her at the end of the driveway, rain dripping off the brim of his rain jacket. He hopped in the car and smiled apologetically. "Sorry about the wet."

"Not a problem. I'll get a towel from the café." Keisha drove down the narrow road while glancing periodically at her cousin. "But why were you standing out there?"

Charlie's handsome dark face turned into a scowl. "Guess I'm just a little worried Mom will come home from her council meeting and find something else for me to do so I can't go to the clinic."

"Last I heard, your mom and dad have an agreement that you can work there as long as your grades are up."

"Right, but with Dad gone . . ." He trailed off and stared out the window at the gray world.

"So you know about—"

"The divorce." He nodded.

"How do you feel about it? I know it's tough."

"Actually, I think it's great." He looked at her now, his young face earnest. "Because my dad is almost free. For as long as I can remember, I've always wondered why he stays. I mean, I love my mom, but like everyone else in this town, I don't like her very much. It always has to be her way, or it's not right, and she can be . . ." He shrugged. "It doesn't matter, but I think maybe both of them will be happier now. Dad deserves it, and maybe she does too." He rubbed a hand over his face. "I think he's been trying to make it work mostly for me, and so many times I've wanted to scream, 'Get out of here, save yourself!'"

He chuckled so she let herself laugh with him. "Anyway, I'm okay. I gotta get through these last years of high school, and then I'll be old enough to do my own thing, no matter what Mom says."

"Your dad supports you wanting to be a vet."

"Yeah. He's great. And they never really fight. But we all know when she's upset."

Keisha knew exactly what he meant. Her aunt's mad face was renowned in their family. "You'll do it, Charlie, and Aunt Olivia will be proud of you eventually."

He shrugged and gave her a grin. "It don't matter. There's worse things."

"Yeah, there are." Like having your parents die or being unhappy all your life. Charlie was a testament to his parents doing something right, but Keisha believed his success was more because of Josiah's influence than Olivia's.

She dropped him off at the vet clinic and watched to make sure he got in. The main vet, Dylan Morgan, usually had farm calls in the morning, but he'd hired another vet to help him with the increasing load. She bet both men were there this rainy morning, and the fact that Charlie wanted to be here rather than sleeping in or watching television said a lot about the way they were training him.

Dread puddled in her stomach as she turned toward the Butter Cake. She was already a little late, but it had been worth it. Maggie would understand. To her relief, Xander's truck wasn't outside in the parking lot, and the dread eased, but that was followed by an odd disappointment. He was gone. Maybe he'd driven the long way back to Panna Creek. Either way, it was no business of hers.

Still, curiosity ate at her. Had he actually become a doctor as

Olivia believed? If so, that meant he hadn't gone to Africa, and the man she knew had been determined to go and do something to make a difference for people the way his grandfather had done.

He'd wanted to do it with her. Had it all been for show?

Struggling with her umbrella, she climbed from the car. When she reached the café, Maggie was in the kitchen. "Hey," she said, smiling at Keisha. "How was your night?"

"Quiet. But at least we didn't lose power."

Maggie laughed. "There's still time. It's supposed to rain all day, but Ronica said Fletcher believes the rain will stop sometime in the night."

"Well, at least that will give us all Friday and Saturday morning to dry out. Maybe we'll have the festival after all. I suppose you heard about the sinkhole at the school?"

"Oh, yes. Cora is overjoyed. She's upstairs working on her costume for the festival. At first, she thought it was all silly, but when she found out how seriously the other girls take it, she's been researching everything about the period. Natalie helped her put the main dress together. Says she has a knack for sewing, just like her youngest daughter."

"That's good. About the dress, I mean." She refrained from asking about Natalie's daughter, Joni. Only Joni's parents believed her drug and alcohol addiction was a medical matter brought on by digestive issues.

"Right." Maggie pursed her lips and looked away, probably thinking along the same lines.

Keisha tied on an apron. "So, did it get busy yesterday?"

"Only a little at lunch and dinner, and this morning around nine, actually. Even after one day, people are going a little stir-crazy with the never-ending rain."

"This morning is when you saw Ronica?"

Maggie nodded and returned to prepping vegetables. "Yes, she came in again. Fletcher is looking poorly, though. It's so sad. Ronica and Fletcher should have decades left together."

"I wish we could do more for her." Keisha hovered near Maggie, trying to concentrate on what task to start first, but her mind wouldn't comply. "Oh, by the way, Ernie came to borrow my ladder yesterday. Apparently, the Greenwoods' roof was leaking a ton of water." There, she hadn't even said Xander's name, but maybe Maggie would hint about where Xander was now.

Maggie stopped cutting. "That old skinflint. Of course he did. I did hear about the leak getting worse, but I hope Ernie didn't go up on the roof."

"No. That was—" Too late, she realized her words would either put her at Xander's house or portray Keisha pumping Ernie for information. "Er, I don't think so."

Maggie rounded on her. "What's wrong?" she asked gently. "Do you want to talk about it? You've been acting weird ever since the rain started. Is it the accident?"

Keisha couldn't help the shudder that rolled through her. "Maybe." Last night, she'd experienced flashbacks of her accident while trying to fall asleep. These vied with the memory of being with Xander on the roof in the rain. Later in her dreams, he'd kissed her, and it was as amazing as it always had been, despite the rain and years between them.

Then he'd pushed her off the roof. Her arms had flailed as she'd fallen, fallen, fallen, never to reach the ground.

"I'm sorry," Maggie said. "But Laina is fine. She's slightly concussed, her arm is definitely broken, and her mother says she must wear a boot for her sprained ankle, but on the whole, she's fine. Doesn't even need to use crutches."

Not like my accident, Keisha thought. Instead of relief, her stomach was knotted. "I'm glad."

"Laina is still saying her gas pedal stuck. They've towed it to a garage to investigate."

Keisha waved a hand. "Laina always drove fast, at least when we were in school."

"Well, having a doctor come on sight when he did was fortuitous."

And just like that they had finally gotten around to Xander. "Doctor?" Keisha asked, her heart giving a slow, painful thump. Olivia's guess had been correct.

Maggie nodded. "You know, Xander used to talk about being interested in medicine when he came in here as a kid, and once when I ran into his mother in Panna Creek, she told me he was studying for that test people have to take to get into med school . . . um, the M-something."

"The MCAT."

"Right, that, but the next time I saw her a few months later, she said he was planning to go to Africa for a while instead like his grandfather. He'd met someone special, and they wanted to change the world. She seemed really happy for him. Allison was always more concerned about her family's happiness than money." Maggie picked up a washed green pepper and began slicing. "But I guess it didn't work out."

More likely, Xander had been leading her on. Maybe he'd even known about her inheritance, which wasn't a million dollars or anything, but it might as well be a million here in Forgotten. "Becoming a doctor was a good fallback," she said bitterly.

"It was at that." Maggie either didn't note Keisha's tone or didn't care to acknowledge it. "Those sisters of his are really cute, but the one is rather a handful."

"They stayed here last night?" It was a normal question, not prying, Keisha assured herself as she forced herself to begin checking their store of butter cakes.

"Right. But he left the girls with Cora to run some errands. He's trying to find someone to fix the leak in his roof. I told him to see Laina's dad at the hardware store. He might have some recommendations."

"There was a lot of water." Keisha counted plenty of butter cakes in the fridge. They rotated them with those in the cupboard as they made fresh ones, so the oldest and yummiest cakes were served first. Maggie must have made the usual yesterday, which meant they didn't need more today unless customer traffic picked up. Tomorrow, they would have plenty of time to make more for the festival if the weather decided to behave.

Maggie put down her knife. "You were there?"

Oops. This time her friend had picked up on her slip. "Uh, yeah. I went to make sure Ernie didn't go out on the roof."

"Good call. It must have been bad. Xander and his sisters came back here soaking wet."

"He'll have a hefty clean-up if he's going to sell." Keisha turned with relief as the bell on the door signaled a customer. "I'll get them."

She hurried out to the counter, but her relief died when she saw Xander coming around the corner to the counter, having apparently come through the rear entrance. His hands were shoved deep into his pockets, his face drawn in a scowl. She knew that expression—he was angry.

"Bad news?" she asked.

He stopped moving, his eyes running from her face down to

her yellow apron and back again. "So you *do* work here. I was beginning to wonder if Maggie was only pulling my leg."

"Yes, I work here." For the first time, she was embarrassed to admit that her dreams of the future had been so utterly wrong. No matter how good Maggie's food was or how much Maggie needed her, this place hadn't been in her plans, and it wasn't where she planned to stay forever.

She found herself wanting to explain about the accident and how even after her body recovered, she'd remained emotionally paralyzed because of the way things had ended. For a year she'd used apathy to cover her heartache. She only started working at the Butter Cake because it was the fastest way to get out of Olivia's house. Because she was no longer in college and receiving money earmarked for her education, the smaller regular monthly allotment from her parents' estate wasn't enough to buy or rent a decent house, even in Forgotten, and Olivia refused to pay out more until Keisha returned to college.

In five more years when Keisha was thirty, Olivia would no longer have any say, but at the time, Keisha had to fight for the agency to choose her path. And she had. Quite possibly, Olivia's insistence about law school might be the reason Keisha was still at the Butter Cake, but that would be childish, and she would never admit such a thing to Xander. Neither did he deserve to know about the rest, especially not about the heartache he'd caused her all those years ago.

His gaze was still fixed on her intently, and she felt heat rising to her face. Why was he staring at her like that?

He rocked back on his heels, hands still in his pockets, his eyes smoldering. "I guess I thought with all the real estate deals you must be working on that you'd have better things to do than to cook and clean up after people." The bitterness in his voice stung her.

"Well, we're not all privileged to be doctors," she snapped. "Or to have former girlfriend's aunts help pay for medical school."

His face flushed. "Is that what this is all about? Payback?"

"Payback for what?" Keisha glared at him. "If you need to pay anyone, it's my aunt." She waved a hand. "Never mind, you do what you want. I don't care."

"No? Well, what about my house? Where does that fit in? I want an explanation."

"I don't owe you anything."

"Of course not. Rich girls like you don't do their own dirty work. You'll send your aunt. Does she collect vintage toy cars now? Or handmade furniture? Looks like she should have been the one fixing my grandfather's roof instead of me."

"Are you insane? We have nothing to do with your house."

"Then explain why *you* purchased it. And why everything I left there now belongs to you."

Denial was on her lips, but before the words could escape her mouth, she remembered Olivia's words about investments. *No, she wouldn't have,* Keisha thought, but Olivia always did as she pleased within certain rules of proper society, most of which Keisha was sure she made up as she went along. This would qualify as proper because it meant making money.

His hands came out of his pockets, and he placed them on the counter between them, leaning forward to stare her down. "I didn't let you steal my future four years ago, and I'm not letting you steal my childhood or my family's past."

The words stung. "I don't want anything from you," she retorted. "In fact, I wish I'd never seen you again!"

"Believe me, the feeling is mutual." Again he gave that bitter, bitter laugh, and his eyes were mocking.

His cold, beautiful eyes. How had she *ever* thought he loved her?

"I-I . . ." But she couldn't talk. She whirled and ran back into the kitchen. She didn't stop under Maggie's stare but continued through the back door and out into the rain, where her tears didn't matter. For the second day in a row, she wasn't going to be responsible. She was going to run away and leave Maggie in the lurch. Maybe she'd drive south and keep on driving until she hit the ocean. She could get a new job and use her savings and monthly allotment from her parents to get a new start.

She picked up speed, reaching the car parked far back in the lot before sense kicked in. No, there was Cupcake, who hated driving in the car; the house she owned and had to pay the mortgage on; and her aunt, who was apparently still playing with her life.

Heart pounding with angry adrenaline, Keisha wrenched open the door and slid inside, jabbing the key into the ignition. That was when the fear hit her—all-encompassing, breath-stealing fear. It blocked out the fury and refused to let her turn the key.

She remembered only too well the anger in her heart on another particular rainy day after Olivia told her that under no circumstance would she approve her marriage to a money-grubbing piece of white trash. Maybe if Keisha hadn't been angry that day, she wouldn't have driven through the night to get back to Xander. Perhaps she might have stopped at the Butter Cake and chatted with Maggie and missed getting in the accident altogether.

She knew it didn't matter, not really. In a way, the accident saved her from worse because Xander didn't come for her, and Olivia was right about him. Still, Keisha wanted nothing to do with Xander's house, not even for money that would add to her independence from Olivia on her thirtieth birthday.

When her racing heartbeat settled into a more normal pattern, she was able to start the engine and drive slowly through the rain to her aunt's house. This time she went all the way down the driveway before remembering that Olivia might not be home. Well, she'd wait. Leaving the car out front, she let herself in through the front door with the key Olivia had given her years ago and insisted she keep.

"Charlie? Is that you?" Olivia's voice floated to her from the direction of the kitchen.

The dragon was home. Time to have it out with the woman, once and for all.

CHAPTER 8

Xander stared after Keisha as she fled into the café kitchen. He wanted to feel triumphant but instead wondered about the tears in her eyes. A pit opened in his stomach. What had he been trying to accomplish? Maybe he'd simply wanted to shake her out of that remote politeness—to make her see *him*.

He also wanted an explanation. He wanted an entire boatload of explanations. Not about the house, but about why she left him. He'd thought the hole in his heart was healed, but at this moment, he knew it was still there, only hidden.

Biting his lip, he shook his head hard, trying to clear it so he could replay their conversation. But he couldn't. All he saw were the tears in her eyes. He had the sudden uneasy feeling that maybe he been so focused on attack and protecting himself that he hadn't tried to listen to what she might have said.

Maggie came from the kitchen door to the right of the counter. "Do you know where Keisha went? Did something happen?"

"But she's just right . . ." He looked past her, trying to see through the doorway.

"She's not there." Maggie stared at him with an odd expression. "There's a back door in the kitchen, and she went right through it. I assume to her car."

"Oh." So Keisha was going to drive in this awful rain in that little car of hers. Because of him.

No, because she'd stolen his house.

Not quite true, of course. His mother had known about the back taxes but hadn't paid. Which meant they had abandoned the house. The fact that he hadn't meant to give up his claim wasn't really the issue. A part of him even hoped Keisha might have purchased his house to save it, but it was clear that wasn't the case. The house was just a money-making deal for her, and it had nothing to do with him. Unless she'd become a better liar since he'd known her.

Or had she been a liar all along?

He felt sick.

"Did she say anything?" Maggie regarded him rather suspiciously.

Guilt assaulted Xander as he mentally replayed the tears welling up in Keisha's hazel eyes. He'd wanted a lot of things over the past four years, but hurting her wasn't one of them.

"Just a minute." He held up a finger to Maggie. "I'll be right back." He turned and sprinted out the back door where he'd left his truck and where he hoped to still find Keisha. Maybe it was all a horrible misunderstanding.

Rain pummeled him, as if someone up in the sky aimed a large hose in his direction. Even a few minutes ago, he'd thought the storm was easing, but now the rain had apparently tripled its efforts. What was it about this crazy weather?

He hurried down the walk that led along the length of the kitchen and the attached garage. Miracles of miracles, her car was still in the parking lot. But even as he waved to catch her attention, she began backing out, her face turned away from him.

Gone.

All the anger drained from his body, or was perhaps washed away by the pouring rain, because it wasn't tears running down his face. Why did he feel like an idiot? So many things he thought they might talk about when they met again, and he'd fallen dreadfully short. If he was honest with himself, which maybe he wasn't when it came to her, in most of his daydreams, she wanted him back, and he always had to tell her that he'd moved on with his life.

Except none of that was true. Not really. Some part of him still longed for her as much as he had the day he first kissed her in St. Louis.

On that magical day, he'd stood there in the university library where they met to study, his heart hammering so hard against his ribcage that he was afraid it would beat right out of his chest, though he knew from all his pre-med classes that such a thing was impossible. Her eyes . . . oh, her eyes. He could drown in them a thousand times and die happy.

Now he had to get past that—he *would* get past it.

His phone began vibrating in his pocket, and with a sigh, he hurried back inside the café and stood dripping by the back door. He checked the screen before answering.

"Hey, Mom. Guess you got my message? The cell phones are working again here."

"For now, they're working, you mean." Her voice sounded faint, as if she were further away than twenty minutes in Panna

Creek. "And to answer your question, yes, I got notices about the property taxes at our apartment, but they were never forwarded here to the house. I thought I had time. I did run into someone from Forgotten, and they mentioned it, but I realized I haven't heard from them since the move, which is why I wanted you to see what was happening. That was last year. I haven't had the energy with the girls and this stupid sickness."

"Well, it's okay, but like I said in my message, the city has sold the house. And maybe that's okay. I know you can use the twenty thousand."

"No! That's your legacy." The tremor in his mother's voice worried him. "The girls have their dad, and you had grandpa." A sigh came through the line. "I'm sorry. I messed it all up."

"Stop. You've had a lot to deal with. We just need to decide what to do here and now."

"I don't want the money. If you don't keep the house, it's still yours. Use it to pay off some of your school debt, or better yet, you should get the house back. Fix it up, and then either live in it or sell it for a profit—you should be able to make much more than twenty thousand from it. And that way you can take as much as you want of the stuff that's still there. I would like to look at it all myself again too, to have a few more things to remember my dad. I left so fast after you graduated. I wasn't really thinking about the future. I just wanted out of there. Away from the ghosts, I suppose. Though with Niles being on the road so much, I probably should have stayed in Forgotten. I had friends there, good people I still miss, but at the time I didn't think I could ever live down my past."

"You could still move back and live in the house yourself."

She laughed. "No, I'm settled now, and I don't want to uproot the girls. The house is yours. It was always meant to be. I told you about the clause in Grandpa's will saying it's yours once you're eighteen—don't you remember? But I haven't seen it in my papers, so maybe it's still at the house in his room."

That meant his grandfather and mother had planned for him to take the house all along, and she wasn't simply saying so because she knew he had a humongous school loan to pay.

"Well, if that's what you want, then I'm going to redeem the house." *Take that, Keisha,* he thought. "But you'll need to transfer the right of redemption to me. Or we need to find that will. I'll figure out what paperwork we need and take off for your place now. It'll take three hours to go the long way, but I know you're missing the girls."

"I really am. Are they missing me?"

"Lila is for sure. Sammy just wants to investigate the house."

She laughed. "Sounds like Sammy. Thanks for taking care of them."

He felt a twinge of guilt since, for the last hour, Maggie's step-daughter had been watching them. "It's been fun but exhausting." No wonder his mother had gone downhill, trying to care for the twins while dealing with her diabetes.

"I know exactly how it is, but don't drive back yet."

"Why not?"

"Because I'm already on my way to you."

"What?" The word shot from him. "You won't get through, especially in your car." Visions of her mired in the flooded road filled his mind. "It'll be worse now. It's still raining like crazy here."

"Of course I'm not going on the regular road." Her tone chided him. "I'm going the long way like I have every time it rains and I need to get to Forgotten."

"Right." He forgot his mother was a native and completely

capable of good decisions. Or at least she was when it didn't involve her diabetes.

"But what if you pass out?"

"Well, that would be a problem, but it's too late now. I actually left two hours ago, during a lull, I might add, so I'll be there in an hour. I knew you might not make it back and bringing the girls home would be a pain, but I can't be without my babies another day. Don't worry. I'm not going to pass out. And if I feel dizzy, I'll stop. I was in bed all day yesterday, and with all the stuff you have me doing, I'm feeling much better."

She did sound better. Brighter somehow. Hopeful. "But—"

"But nothing. I'll meet you at the Butter Cake for a late lunch, and then I'll take the girls over to my friend's house. She said we could stay with her tonight. You too, if you want."

"I'll keep my room at the Butter Cake." He didn't relish the idea of staying at a stranger's. "But if I can get all this house stuff wrapped up, I'll follow you home in the morning." It might take longer, though, especially if he couldn't convince the city council to lower the overdue tax fees. After four years of struggling through medical school and accumulating more debt than he could have ever imagined at the outset, he didn't have a lot of room to borrow more funds, even on his future earnings.

"No hurry on my account," she said. "I'm not going home tomorrow."

Water dripped from his hair into his eyes, and he wiped it away. "Why not? The rain will probably stop by then."

"Of course it will. But this weekend is Forgotten's Harvest Festival, and the girls and I always go back for that. I've brought their pioneer costumes."

"It's way too wet for any festival." If she could see the little streams running into the gutters on Main as he had on his way back from the hardware store, she wouldn't even consider going.

"Oh, there will be a festival. There always is. You'll see. It'll dry out enough." She lowered her voice. "They have to."

"What do you mean?" He vaguely remembered something odd surrounding the festival, but why did she sound so eerie?

"Well, the one time the town didn't have the festival—that was before I was born—there was a drought, and it ruined the following year's harvest. People said it was because the town didn't hold the reenactment of the town's founding, so Chelsea Morgan's ghost didn't come to walk and sing over the fields."

"Oh, come on," he said. "You're talking about the woman who gave up all comfort to marry the man she loved and who helped everyone who came to town." Every school child in Forgotten and Panna Creek knew of the generosity of both Chelsea and James Morgan, the founders of Forgotten. "I seriously doubt she'd try to cause a drought, alive or dead."

"I know it's silly," she said, laughing again. "But that's how it is in a small town. So there will be a festival, even if it's a soggy one. Don't be surprised when the ghost of Chelsea Morgan makes things work out after all."

He shook his head. "And here I thought it was God who answered prayers."

"Yes, Him too. But she'll put in a good word for us."

"I hope you're not taking anything except the meds I prescribed."

"I'm all right, son." Amusement laced her words. "In fact, I have some fantastic news to tell you. By the way, I'm bringing some of Niles' clothes for you. See you soon." Before he could get in another word, she hung up.

He sighed, pushing his worry to the back of his mind. His

mother was a full-grown woman, and she knew her own mind. Besides, he'd seen the snail's pace at which she drove in the rain. She should be fine, though it was unlikely she'd be here before another two hours.

Meanwhile, he couldn't possibly hope to hear from the town council about his tax petition before late afternoon. Penny would call if they decided anything.

And what if they dragged it out? Well, there was nothing he could do about that.

What he could do was return to the house and make sure the temporary repairs were holding. He could also look for a will and get his cars—and maybe a few of his grandfather's. Just in case. Even if he'd technically be trespassing, it wasn't stealing because he planned to redeem the house as soon as he got the loan to pay the back taxes. As a double plus, Sammy would be able to look around and get it out of her system. What could happen?

Inside the house, Maggie was nowhere to be seen at the counter, so he headed upstairs. The girls were in the room staring at the television again while the round-faced teen, Cora, focused on a mound of blue material in her hands, her long brown hair spilling over her shoulders.

"Oh, good, you're back," she said loudly over the sound of the television, deftly tying off her thread. "I need to go ask Maggie something." She shook out the dress. "Does it look like something Chelsea Morgan would wear? It's too late this year, but I hope next year, I'll get to play her as a young girl in the reenactment."

He contemplated the dress that looked like a newer, more colorful version of something that might be worn by a frontier woman in the 1860s. "It's really nice. But you think there's even going to be a harvest festival with all this rain?" He handed her a twenty for watching the girls.

"Thank you. The rain's going to stop before morning. Fletcher Wilson says so. He might not be all there, but everyone says he's always right. Besides, if we don't have it, bad things will happen."

"Like what?" Sammy turned from the television, her eyes wide.

"I don't know. I'm new here," Cora said with a grin.

Sammy's stare went to him. "You should know. You grew up here."

"Something about a drought," he said with a shrug. "It's just a legend. Look, guess what? We're going back to the house to explore. And Mom's on her way. Apparently, she loves this festival—or she's missing you guys."

"Good, I miss her too," Lila said. "And see?" she added to her sister, "I told you we went to the festival before. I remember people running down the street with potatoes."

Cora gathered her dress and headed for the door. "It's people singing as they gather boxes and bags of food set out for the poor. Potatoes too, I guess, if they grow them here."

"Well, I don't remember." Sammy frowned and jumped from the bed. "Let's go to the house now. I'm bored of watching TV."

"Have fun. See you later." With a little wave, Cora disappeared into the hallway.

"Is it still raining?" Lila asked, looking toward the shuttered window.

"Yes. Obvi." Sammy pointed to Xander's wet hair.

"Can't you hear it?" Xander could, even above the sound of the TV. He grabbed the remote and lowered the sound.

"Yeah," Lila said. "Then I don't want to go to the house. Can I stay here with Maggie and Cora?"

"I'll find all Grandpa's treasure myself," Sammy said, sniffing her offense.

"There's no treasure, is there?" Lila asked him.

"Not that I'm aware of."

"Sure there is," Sammy insisted. "Grandpa went to Africa, and everyone knows there's plenty of gold in Africa. I saw so on the TV. He probably brought home a whole suitcase of it."

Once again, Lila turned to him. "Is that right? Is there lots of gold in Africa?"

Where did kids get this stuff? "I'm sure there's gold in Africa, but I don't know if Grandpa ever found or bought any. He never showed any to me." Then, because Sammy's face was crestfallen, he added, "But that doesn't mean there isn't another kind of treasure. Who knows what we'll find? Some of Grandpa's car collection has to be really antique by now, and any of the older toys he gave me from his childhood as well. Even my old cars are probably vintage." He laughed because he didn't really know at what point things became vintage or antique. "And I remember my grandmother used to like little silver spoons. I don't know what might have happened to them, though. She died when I was about your age."

"Silver spoons?" Lila said. "I would love those. Okay, I'll go."

Sammy smirked. "Oh, now you believe me."

"First, grab those umbrellas Maggie lent us." Xander stepped between them. "I don't want you wet."

Sammy rolled her eyes. "You're already wet. Why didn't you use them?"

"Because I had other things on my mind." Or one thing, rather—Keisha.

They made it out to the truck without getting wet. The wind had died down, and he was sure the rain was lighter now. But when they arrived at the house, there was a sign on the door that read *No Trespassing,* and the key no longer opened the lock.

"Uh-oh," Sammy said. "I think the lady who stole your house is trying to keep us out."

Lila nodded solemnly. "She must want Grandma's spoons."

"And the gold," Sammy agreed.

Clearly, the girls had been listening when he'd left the message to their mother. He went from calm to seeing red in the space of a single heartbeat. That was it. He was going to have it out with Keisha—and maybe with her aunt as well.

"Come on," he growled. "We'll go back to the Butter Cake and wait for Mom."

"Can we get pizza?" Sammy asked. "I'm starving, and Maggie's food's good, but Cora says Maggie doesn't cook pizza."

"Yeah, we can get pizza." Breakfast had been too early to wait any longer for their lunch, despite what his mother wanted. But one way or the other, as soon as he delivered the girls to her, he was getting inside *his* house.

Today.

CHAPTER 9

Keisha stared at her aunt in disbelief. "I can't believe you bought his house."

Olivia sipped from a steaming cup as she stood on the other side of her substantial island counter in her very white and pristine kitchen. "Well, officially, it wasn't his house, but his mother's, and now it belongs to the city since she defaulted for ten years on the taxes. She was notified. There's proof of that."

"But knowing about us . . . how could you?" Keisha's stomach churned with acid.

"How could I not? If I didn't act, someone else in this town certainly would have. And why should someone else receive the benefit? We can easily double our investment, even with the repairs. We weren't allowed to go inside the house until after the auction, but I had someone investigate the outside, and it's sturdy." The note of pride in her voice was unmistakable.

"Except the roof is leaking, and now the carpet has to be replaced."

Oliva made a slight utterance and waved the concern away. "The carpet was always going to be replaced. I had someone out there this morning, and there was some wet carpet but nothing leaking."

"That's because Xander went up on the roof and stopped it." Her aunt could be so obtuse sometimes.

Olivia's eyes narrowed. "I thought you were going to stay away from him."

"I told you that *after* Ernie borrowed my ladder to lend to Xander so he could fix the roof. But what does it matter if I see him? Unless doctors can also be white trash." Keisha tilted her head. "Oh, wait, a doctor is what you want Charlie to be, isn't it? So I guess it's only the color of Xander's skin that makes him unacceptable."

Olivia set her cup down, her back stiffening. She was still wearing heels, and that made her a good three inches taller than Keisha, able to effectively look down at her with more than her customary haughtiness. "Since when do you talk to me like that? I saw the way that boy broke your heart. Don't think I don't know why you refuse to give any serious thought to any of those attorneys who keep asking you out."

"It has nothing to do with Xander. I simply don't care about the law anymore." There, she'd said it. "And I don't want to marry someone who will be talking about it. So which is it?" Keisha pressed on. "Is Xander still on your hit list because he's white trash or because his mother had him out of wedlock? What about you and the relationship you're having with your online friend?"

"I would never cheat," Olivia spat, hurt in her eyes.

"No. I guess that's why it's time for the divorce." Keisha felt suddenly deflated. No matter how disagreeable she found Olivia, she didn't want to hurt her aunt, if only because of her uncle and Charlie. Well, or Charlie, rather. She supposed she didn't have to hold back on Josiah's account anymore.

"Would it make a difference if you knew that Xander Greenwood made an application to the city council to waive the non-payment fees related to his house?" Olivia asked. "Can you believe the gall of that man? They know about property taxes, so why should they get a pass?" She sniffed. "Maybe he's *not* really a doctor. He could have dropped out. If he were a real doctor, he wouldn't even sneeze at that sort of money."

"Even those who have just finished medical school? Or have you been paying for his sixty-five thousand dollar tuition every year, plus room and board?" Keisha had looked up general costs last night after Olivia told her about the money, and the idea that Xander had finished medical school despite the insurmountable costs was impressive.

"Of course not." Olivia picked up her cup, a slight tremor in her hand. "Well, unless there are some extenuating circumstances he can prove, our answer will have to be no to waiving any fees. He won't be getting back in the house until he pays them and redeems the property. By the way, I had the doors rekeyed this morning. I did a walk-through last week, and I believe the abandoned items will sell for enough to cover most of the repairs."

"But those items belonged to his family." Had Xander known about the key when they last talked? He hadn't mentioned it, only her purchase of the property. Either way, he had a right to be angry, though it wasn't her fault, or really even her aunt's. His mother had faulted on the property. Did he expect everyone in town to roll out the red carpet for him just because he had become a doctor?

"No, everything in that house belongs to you."

"Then give me the key," Keisha surprised herself by saying.

Olivia blinked. "I won't."

"It's my house, isn't it?"

"It's *our* house."

"Did you buy it with the money my dad left or with some of your own?"

Olivia's chin lifted. "My funds are currently all invested, so yes, I purchased it on your behalf, but since I control the funds until you're thirty or married to someone of whom I approve, it's my house, not yours." The telltale raising of her voice signaled her upset. "And you'd better not dare accuse me of mishandling your funds because I have made you a significant amount since my brother's death, and as your agent, the very tiny percentage I make on the increases barely covers my time. I consider this a sacred trust. Talk to your accountant if you don't believe me."

"I don't need to." Even if Keisha didn't know that Olivia was a stickler for rules, she trusted her independent accountant, a long-time friend of her parents who happened to dislike Olivia immensely. "But I want the key. I'm going to let Xander take whatever he wants from the house."

Olivia's jaw clenched and unclenched in an apparent effort to remain calm. "Well, I don't have it yet. I ordered it last night after talking to you, and it was done this morning—to preserve our interests, I might add. I'll be picking up the key whenever this infernal rain ends, and you can have it if you want, but I think you're making a mistake. Wait a week, and this will all blow over. Trust me."

More tears threatened to overflow Keisha's eyes, but she

blinked them back and picked up her keys from the counter. "He's angry. I don't think this is going to blow over."

She snorted. "Those kinds of people always blame someone else for their actions, or lack of actions in this case."

Keisha wanted to say, "You don't know him like I used to," but she couldn't. Because, in the end, she hadn't known Xander at all. "How did you know he had been accepted to med school?" The thought of the three thousand dollars Olivia had given him weighed her down.

"He told me. I think in an attempt to impress me. And before you ask, the money didn't come from your funds, though it was from funds your father left to me. I've always felt I also needed to use those for your welfare."

Which might explain the lavish gifts Olivia often bestowed on her—mostly clothes or furniture designed to increase their standing in the community. As Josiah mentioned, dressing people was one of her gifts.

Three thousand dollars was a little low for the medical school deposits Keisha had seen online, which were normally due in March or April before the start of school in the fall. But Xander didn't have that kind of money in his account when she left. They'd counted up everything to prepare for the expenses in Africa not covered by their sponsor. Without her funds, he probably still could have found a way to go to Africa, but with Olivia's money, he'd certainly had enough. So why hadn't he gone?

Maybe he never planned to go. Maybe medical school was the plan all along, especially if he married her and had access to her inheritance.

Stop, she told herself. It really didn't matter. She had to let it go now. Three thousand was a small price to pay compared to years of pain. For all their differences, she had Olivia to thank for saving her from that, even if it came at such an emotional cost.

"I'll come back later for the key," she said. "Right now, I have to go to work." Without waiting for a response, she ran from the room. Guilt about leaving the café without talking to Maggie had been eating at her during the entire conversation. Being irresponsible wasn't like her—until Xander had walked back into her life.

Outside, the rain seemed to have lightened since she arrived, but it was windier now. Not good. Too often here in Forgotten when the wind and rain came together, it meant the electricity went off.

When she arrived at the café, Xander's truck was nowhere to be seen, which was good because she didn't want to face his anger, especially when she had no key to give him.

Maggie was in the kitchen making sandwiches. She stared hard at Keisha. "Want to tell me what's going on? Are you fighting with Xander Greenwood?"

"I . . . uh . . . I guess a little." Keisha stared sheepishly at the ground. She was being a little bit of an idiot, but Xander pushed all the wrong buttons.

Maggie shook her head sympathetically. "Do you want to talk about it?"

"No." Keisha said and then added almost immediately, "Yes."

Maggie topped the sandwiches with a slice of her homemade bread. "Okay, I'll take this out to our only lunch customers so far, and I'll be right back. Maybe you could dish out some butter cake for them? I'm selling it for half price today. We don't want it to go to waste."

"Right. Sure." Keisha followed her out to the counter to

see Easton and Ashton Ramos, two old Forgotten ranchers, ensconced in their usual seat by a window. She was surprised they'd ventured so far from their property today, but maybe the rain left them with little they could do. Perhaps one day of staying indoors had bored them. She hoped that would be the case with the farmers and construction workers in town as well, for Maggie's bottom line.

Her thoughts turned out to be prophetic a short time later when a large group of construction workers came in laughing and shaking off the rain. She took their orders while Maggie brought out the mop to clean up their drips. Keisha had barely finished with them when two more groups came in. Attorneys this time, and several store owners.

Maggie grinned at her, mouthing *sorry*. But Keisha wasn't unhappy. Maybe it was best *not* to tell Maggie about her past with Xander. She'd probably urge her to talk to him.

As the construction workers left, more locals came in, adults and teens, everyone talking about Laina's accident, Xander Greenwood being back, and what might happen if the weather didn't clear in time for the Harvest Festival on Saturday. The consensus seemed to be that they'd gather food for the poor down Main Street as usual, but they'd forego the booths and games and move straight to the reenactment at a local barn that was now used only for wedding parties in the winter. Refreshments would be provided by everyone in attendance.

Ronica Wilson came in and overheard someone suggesting this for the tenth time. "Oh, no," she said. "It's going to be fine. In fact, Fletcher says to expect a heatwave. Everyone got their costumes ready?"

Cora and a group of teens waved their hands. "We can do the whole festival in the rain," one of them shouted.

Ronica beamed at them proudly. "That's the spirit. But no need. You'll see."

Keisha was pouring more coffee and hot chocolate in the dining section near the rear entrance when Xander entered with his little sisters. He carried a pizza box, but from the smears on the little girls' faces, they'd already eaten their share. She opened her mouth to say something, but they passed without speaking and went up the stairs. Xander still looked angry. As Keisha stared after them, Sammy turned and stuck her tongue out at Keisha. Which meant he'd told them about her owning the house. She suspected they'd also learned about the changed locks.

Fine, she thought, *be that way.* If the man couldn't be civil, then she certainly wouldn't go out of her way to smooth things over. What had she ever seen in him anyway? Who cared about broad shoulders, sexy blond hair, and beautiful eyes? Who cared about a smile that made her stomach tighten and a million butterflies take flight? Honesty and trust were far more important.

Still, a little more of her heart crumbled, which was silly and ridiculous and utterly sad.

"Hey, Keisha."

She turned to see Jeremy Wilson, Ronica and Fletcher's son, who now ran their farm and had recently built a new house next to his parents'—to help land him a wife, according to town rumor. She'd known him all her life, though they'd never dated. He'd been trying to change that, but her heart wasn't in it. He was good looking and strong, with blond hair—bleached almost white now by the sun—and blue eyes. He grew corn and alfalfa and would probably never leave his wife. But with him, there were no butterflies or daydreams.

"Hey, Jeremy," she said.

"You volunteering at the dunking booth again this year?" he asked with a grin.

"What, so you can dunk me five times again? Not on your life. I'm actually in charge of it, so I made sure I was not on the volunteer list."

He chuckled. "Well then, maybe the kissing booth." He waggled his eyebrows. "Remember, it's for a good cause."

She laughed and slugged his arm. "Dream on."

"Well, if you are, I'll be there." With a tip of his cowboy hat, he headed toward the back door, where he held the door open for a woman she recognized: Xander's mother, Alison Greenwood Tyler.

The few times they'd crossed paths here in the café or in Panna Creek. Keisha had always wanted to ask her about Xander, but her pride hadn't let her. Today, her smile froze on her face as she wondered if Alison might stop and talk to her, if however briefly. Had Xander told his mother about her involvement in the house?

But Alison only nodded briefly as her eyes went past Keisha to someone behind her. Xander. Of course he'd come back down to meet his mother.

Without looking again at either of them, Keisha gripped her coffee pot and returned to the counter. Maggie was taking more orders, so Keisha grabbed the slips and hurried to the back to start cooking. Usually, she was in the front, but they took turns often enough that Maggie might not realize it was because of Xander. She only had to hold out until closing time at seven, and then she could go home.

Xander stared after Keisha, the tension in his body so great he found it hard to think. Earlier with the girls, he'd taken the coward's way out and hurried past her, pretending he didn't see her and using what he told himself was a lot of restraint. He didn't want to see any more tears, even if she had temporarily locked him out of his own house.

He'd barely made it to his room when his mom texted that she'd arrived, so he came downstairs just in time to witness some kind of intimacy between Keisha and Jeremy Wilson. They'd been laughing, and at one point, she'd laid her hand on his arm.

Irritation rippled through Xander, but he couldn't pinpoint why. Keisha was a free woman he had no claim on, and Jeremy Wilson had been a decent guy in high school, unlike his two older brothers, both of whom had been jocks and colossal jerks. Was Jeremy part of the reason Keisha was still in Forgotten? Could be, though they didn't appear to be a couple.

He dragged his attention from the direction Keisha had disappeared to where his mother stood, but somehow he still felt Keisha in the café, working out of his line of sight. Had she even noticed him? He couldn't help wondering why she'd become emotional this morning when he confronted her. Was it because he embarrassed her or because . . . No, she didn't still care. Maybe she never had. He had to face the harsh reality that there was nothing for him here, no future, at least. There was only the house and his past.

Still, he wished he'd simply asked her this morning if he could buy a few of his family's belongings instead of pushing so hard. The woman he'd loved would have given them freely. Instead, he'd let his hurt and anger take over, which was yet another sign that he wasn't over Keisha, not by a long shot. And he had to get over her, sooner rather than later. They didn't have to be friends, but their paths would occasionally cross with him working in

Panna Creek. If he decided to stay in Forgotten or Panna Creek after residency for some reason, he'd have to adjust to seeing her with someone else and watch her raise a family that wasn't also his.

Why did the thought hurt so much?

Pasting a smile on his face, he greeted his mother. "About time," he teased.

"Well, with all that talk about passing out, I wanted to be careful." She rolled her eyes. "How are the girls?"

"Fine, but to give you fair warning, they already ate. Pizza."

She laughed. "Good. I stopped for food in the last town over. Didn't want my blood sugar to get too low."

"Have you tested since you left Panna Creek?"

"No, but I feel good."

"That can be deceptive."

"Right, but there's something—" She broke off, looking around at the tables near them in an apparent attempt to check for listening ears. But the rush hour—if there had been one—was over, and the table nearest them was empty. "There's something more to all this stuff than we thought, and only yesterday did I figure it out. I know why it's been so bad now. I'm pregnant." Her voice was constrained, but he could sense emotion begging to burst through.

"Pregnant?" If someone said it had suddenly stopped raining water and was now dropping pizza, he couldn't have been more surprised. "But I thought you were going through menopause."

"That's what my doctor thought three months ago when I went to see him."

"He didn't give you a pregnancy test?"

"We were focused on the diabetes."

Only in a small town, he thought a little disparagingly. "Okay, so how do you feel about this? It's good, right?" he hazarded a guess.

Her face lit up. "It's wonderful! I thought it was only diabetes these past three months, but now I think the pregnancy is what made it flare up so bad in the first place." There was no hiding the emotion now, and he could name it: joy. "I can't wait to tell Niles. Oh, I hope it's another boy. I know he'd like a son."

"I need to do a full workup on you. Not only because of your diabetes, but because of your age." Xander mentally calculated all the things that could go wrong with her pregnancy. The first thing he would do would be to make sure the meds she was on were okay for pregnancy.

"I know, forty-two is ancient in baby land. But I got a late start. Well, except for you."

"Sixteen *was* a little too young." Worry ate at him.

Her brow furrowed. "I know that tone. Come on, be happy for me."

"I am, really." He smiled. "The girls will be happy too. Congratulations." He choked a little on the words, thinking how odd it was to be saying those words to his mother. In another life, it might be his wife with a baby on the way. At twenty-eight, he might not be ready to be a parent, but he'd begun to think about starting a family with a woman he could trust with his heart.

"The girls will be in absolute *heaven*," she corrected. "Lila always asks for a baby sister or brother for Christmases and birthdays, and every other holiday as well."

"There might be complications."

She laughed and hugged him. "That's what I have you for. My doctor son. You can do all the tests you want, and I'll listen to your advice." She arched a brow. "But just so you know, for the actual prenatal visits and such, I'm going to have the same midwife I had with the girls."

He leaned over and kissed the top of her head. "That's probably a good idea. I've only helped deliver two babies so far. As long as I can do a full blood workup and be sure no one is missing anything, I don't care who you choose. Midwives generally have excellent results."

"I know. Come on. Let's go tell the girls. Niles is on standby to video chat with us for the big announcement so he won't miss their reactions."

He went upstairs with her, his mind drifting back to Keisha. Where had she gone this morning after their confrontation? Had it been to meet Jeremy somewhere, or had she gone to make sure the house was locked up and her interests protected?

As they reached the room, his phone dinged with a message, and he opened it hurriedly to see that it was Penny from town hall. It read: *The storm and everything going on with a sinkhole in front of the school has the council running around like crazy, but they did finally discuss your situation. Unfortunately, it's bad news. They denied your request to waive the penalty taxes. Please let me know if you plan to appeal their decision or if you have changed your mind about redeeming the house.*

This meant that to redeem the house, he'd have to defer his loans and apply for another one, as well as use his credit card. Unless he could convince Keisha to let him search the house for any evidence to submit. Would she allow it? The old Keisha would have.

Whatever happened, he almost wished he'd gone to that fancy hospital in LA and never come back to Forgotten.

Almost.

Because running away wasn't something his grandfather would be proud of, and he'd worked all his life to make the old man proud. He would stay to fight.

CHAPTER 10

Keisha threw herself into cooking in the kitchen, trying not to think about Xander. In her mind, she confronted him a dozen times, but the vision of him walking past her in the cafe without looking her way made the mental confrontations fall flat.

Maggie came into the back for orders. "Guess who's out there?"

Keisha's stomach tightened so much it hurt. "Who?" Her voice was faint, but Maggie didn't seem to notice.

"Laina, with an arm cast and a boot. Ayleen Jenkins drove her over. And apparently, the mechanic looked at her car, and there was something wrong with the gas line. It stuck open. She was lucky it didn't happen further into town—we're all lucky. She could have easily run into someone or one of the buildings."

Keisha shuddered. "How scary."

"That Beetle was ancient. She's going to buy another one. Thankfully a much newer model."

Keisha heard the approval in Maggie's voice. Getting right back on the horse after a fall was a theme for Forgotten. For everyone except Keisha apparently. "Good for her," she said, meaning it.

In the end, Maggie let Keisha go home early because the wind was picking up and the customers stopped coming. "Time to hunker down," Maggie told her. "The worst should blow over tonight."

Keisha pulled on her jacket, but Maggie wasn't finished. "What were you going to tell me before everyone started coming in? Talk while I dish up some leftovers for you to take home. You didn't take your break."

"I did earlier when I left."

"You didn't eat." Maggie began piling steak and rice into a container. "Well?"

Keisha debated. Since coming to work here, Maggie was the closest thing she had to a best friend, but what would it help talking about Xander now? Nothing. Yet she had to tell someone because having only Olivia know about Xander was tearing her apart—Olivia, who believed the worst and had been right.

Keisha sat on the closest chair at the little table. "When I was in St Louis at the university, I . . . Xander and I dated. I was the woman he told his mom about. At least I think I was." Maybe there was someone else. She could no longer say for sure. "We were planning to elope and go to Africa and build a village, and then . . ."

Maggie drew in a swift breath. "The accident! Oh, Keisha, I'm so sorry."

"Don't be. There's more, but suffice it to say that, in the end, he needed a deposit for medical school, and Olivia gave it to him on the condition that he'd leave me alone. And he did."

"Oh, honey." Maggie dropped her fork and hugged her tightly.

"What a rotten thing to do. Sounds just like Olivia." She paused, still holding Keisha. "Sorry, I shouldn't have said that, but still."

Keisha hiccupped a laugh that was half a sob. "That's okay. We both know it's true, and now you know about Xander. When I look at him . . . well, it's awkward."

"Makes me want to go up there and kick him out," Maggie grumbled.

Tears bit at Keisha's eyes. "No, don't," she said, stepping back. "I'm over him. Except that's not all. Olivia bought his house at auction last week, and now Xander thinks I'm responsible."

"That's crazy but good." Maggie grabbed another container for vegetables. "Kind of ironic if you ask me."

"No, it's not good. I think he thinks I did it on purpose."

Maggie groaned. "Oh, I guess I can see that. Well, he should be gone soon. And don't worry, while he's here, you can work in the kitchen as much as you want."

Ah, so she had noticed. "Thanks, Maggie."

Maggie grinned and handed her the food containers. "Whatever you do, remember I love you. You are amazing, and I know I'm incredibly lucky to have you working here. Even once you get moving on to whatever else you decide to do, you will always be one of my dearest friends."

It was exactly what Keisha needed to hear—that she was loved and had a future. Even if that future was without Xander. Yes, it was time to continue moving forward. "Thanks. That means a lot. I think I'm almost ready. By April, I should finish my online classes for my economics degree, but I'll stay here until then."

"That'll give us plenty of time to go through a few people to find the right replacement," Maggie said. "I might need two workers to replace you, though," she added with a laugh.

Keisha stepped outside, feeling stronger than she had all day. Instantly, the wind tugged at her jacket, and her carefully twisted hair threatened to burst free. At least it was warmer than it had been earlier. Even the raindrops that were still coming down, stinging as they hit her face, felt warm. She hurried to the car, glancing back at the windows of the café. If Xander weren't staying another night, she'd be tempted to remain at the Butter Cake with Maggie instead of trying to get back home. Cupcake would be okay inside her house alone until morning. But Xander was still there, even though his mother and the girls had apparently gone to a friend's.

Pushing the thought aside, she concentrated on driving home slowly, breaking for the occasional branch or debris that blew across the road. At home, she found an envelope taped to her door, and trepidation roared to life inside her. Could it be some kind of summons from Xander? As she opened it, standing there on her wet porch, her hand shook slightly. Inside was a key. Nothing more, not even a note, but Keisha knew Olivia was responsible for sending someone to leave it there. She hadn't come personally, or there would have been an accompanying snarky message. Keisha almost blessed the wind and rain for that.

Inside, her house was hot because she'd pushed up the heat last night when the chill wouldn't leave her, and she didn't wait to get to her bedroom to start shedding her white work blouse. Upstairs, she slid into her only remaining clean clothes—a wrinkled, hot pink T-shirt and her favorite jean shorts—or rather, what used to be her favorite shorts. Not too tight or loose, worn to the point of soft comfort, the kind that made her backside look perfect. Her mother had bought them for her in Lincoln during her last year of high school, and she'd worn them every time the weather permitted. She'd even been wearing them on the night of the fire.

Every woman she knew longed for similar shorts, and Keisha had never found a better pair. She was looking, however, because ever since the accident, these were too short to wear in public, especially when she sat. They showed far too much of the ugly scar slicing haphazardly across her leg, and now she only wore them when she was alone or had nothing else clean.

Her hand went instinctively to the bottom of the scar, tracing its terrible path. Maybe she should try the surgery. If it helped with the tightness and bumpiness, that alone might remove some of her self-consciousness. However, the idea of going through more surgery made her remember the nightmare of waking up groggy and alone in the hospital. No parents, no Xander, no one. Not even Olivia.

She pulled her fingers away and concentrated on enjoying the comfort of the shorts, like a virtual hug from her mother. She needed that comfort now. That and food, and a night of good sleep. She followed her growling stomach back to her entryway, where she'd left the takeout bags on the end table near her loveseat. Cupcake hurried ahead of her and began meowing at the door.

"You don't want to go out there," Keisha told her. "Use the litter box."

Cupcake ran over and brushed up against her, meowing louder.

"Okay, okay." Keisha knew Cupcake wouldn't stop until she got what she wanted, so she'd go outside with her, but not without a leash. Not in this wind. Small cats were too easily hurt by falling objects.

She grabbed the harness from the end table by the loveseat and snapped it on. Cupcake arched her back in offense, and Keisha didn't blame her because usually she had free run of the yard and beyond, but they'd used it enough that the cat soon settled down to a mild distaste. "Sorry, but I don't want to lose you in this storm."

At least the cat shouldn't last long out in the rain. Keisha opened the door to peek out, and Cupcake zipped through the opening, pulling her along. "Wait, my jacket," she said as Cupcake fought to get to the carport.

Nixing the idea of the jacket, Keisha pulled the door shut and hurried along with her. The feline didn't stop at the carport, instead pulling toward the thick stand of lilac bushes along the property line. Rain pelted Keisha's face, still those strangely warm droplets. She lifted her eyes to the dark sky, watching the billowing gray clouds that were both beautiful and a little terrifying. Abruptly, lightning flashed, and thunder cracked too soon afterward for comfort, startling both her and the cat.

"Cupcake!" she shouted as the feline pulled the leash from her hand and disappeared into the bush altogether. "Get out here! Come on. We have to get inside. That lightning is really close."

But wherever she was, Cupcake was too scared now to come out, which meant Keisha would have to go in after her. Getting down on her hands and knees in the wet grass, she called, "Here kitty, kitty, kitty, kitty, kitty, kitty, kitty, kitty, kitty, kitty" all in one breath as her mother had done with one of Cupcake's progenitors when she was a child. "Come on, sweetie." Why, oh why had she let the cat out at all?

Keisha was halfway inside a bush, using her phone flashlight to search for the end of the leash, when footsteps made her begin to back up. But the branches caught in her hair, pulling painfully. "Just great," she muttered.

"Keisha, what are you doing?" The shouted words came to her from out of nowhere. "Do you know you left your door open?"

The noise of the storm was such that she hadn't heard anyone approaching, but she'd know that voice anywhere. Here she was on her hands and knees with her hair caught in the branches, so of course, it was *him*.

It was a perfectly rotten end to a rotten day.

Overhead, lightning flashed again.

CHAPTER 11

After his mother and the twins left the Butter Cake Café, Xander began to stew. Why had the council rejected his case? And what had Penny meant by an appeal? He decided to call and ask.

"I was just about to call you," she said when she answered. "I wasn't sure if you got my message."

"Sorry for not responding earlier. I was occupied. But I got the message. What do you mean by appeal?"

"First, let me say again that I'm really sorry. But the council's reasoning is that unless you can show extenuating circumstances, then you are liable for the fees and interest."

"What kind of extenuating circumstances?" Would medical school count? What about his mother's sickness?

"Well, like the owner wasn't notified or that we had the wrong listed owner. That sort of thing. Something that could be argued. They might not waive them entirely, but they could. Or they might opt to allow payment with no interest. You mentioned during one of our other conversations that your grandfather meant to leave the house to you and not to your mother. Can you or your mother prove that? Then we'll have notified the wrong person about the taxes."

"My mother is in town now. Can she sign an affidavit or something?"

"I doubt that will help." Her voice lowered confidentially, "You probably don't know this, but Olivia Campbell is on the city council. Mostly because everyone loves her husband, and she campaigns like crazy. A lot of the members vote with her."

"Isn't that a conflict of interest? She should recuse herself."

"Well, technically, it's her niece who bought the house, and the redemption isn't connected . . . exactly."

"You know it is. The more money I have to come up with, the more she'll stand to gain—the more they both stand to gain."

"Look, I shouldn't be saying this, but I think you should talk to Keisha. She's a really nice girl, and reasonable. And since she's the listed owner, she could go a long way toward swaying Olivia. She has always considered Keisha her daughter, especially since the accident."

Which made no sense to Xander since back when he'd known Keisha, she and her aunt had not gotten along. He always had the feeling she tried to stay as far away from Olivia as possible.

But maybe he'd read *that* wrong too.

"I'm still going to redeem the house," he said, knowing he sounded a little angry.

Penny's chuckle sounded loud in his ear. "I know, but maybe it's better not to advertise that so loudly. Because then there will be no incentive for the council, you know? If you have any intention of living there, even for a short time, it might help your appeal. Having another doctor in town is something everyone has wanted, but if they think it's a done deal, they have less incentive to waive some of those fees."

"Even when I redeem the house, it doesn't mean I'll be living in it." He didn't mean the words to come out as a growl.

"Well, residency is four years, isn't it?" Penny said cheerfully. "So it's possible you'll be around for that long."

He stifled a sigh. "I guess." He'd planned to go to LA after the first year when his mother should be back on track, but now with the new baby, she might need help a little longer. He made his voice more congenial. "Thanks, Penny. You've been nicer than you had to be. I appreciate it."

"You're welcome." The warmth in her voice was unmistakable. "Anytime. I have a daughter around your age, and I always hope people will be around to help her when she needs it. And speaking of that, do you remember a girl named Ayleen from high school? Ayleen Jenkins?"

He was drawing an utter blank, which only told him that Ayleen likely hadn't been in his grade, or they'd run in different circles. Not everyone had stood out like Keisha. "Um, I don't know," he said. "It's been a long time."

"Well, I'll have to reintroduce you." Penny chuckled again. "But I'd better go now. I'm off, and the wind out there is picking up."

"Sorry to keep you." The wind was howling fiercely outside, and was that thunder he heard? "Thanks."

He hung up and went to the window. Across the street was a quaint brick church with a beautiful spire. It was the sort of church everyone expected to find in a small town, except right now, with the dark, billowing clouds, it looked more ominous than comforting. Or maybe that was because he was suddenly remembering his grandpa's funeral there and his secret vow to leave town and see the world to follow in his footsteps. Yet here he was in Forgotten again, never having left the United States and without seeing much more than St. Louis and Washington DC where he went to medical school.

He changed into a set of clothing his mother had brought him. Niles was a little smaller than he was in the chest, so the green T-shirt was tight, but it was spandex, so it didn't really matter. The pants fit well enough, and for the first time in two days, he felt completely dry.

That meant it was time to face Keisha. Only this time, he'd keep his cool and ask her calmly about possible documents. No need to break in yet if she'd give him the key.

Maggie was wiping the counter as he came downstairs to an eerily empty café. Not even her husband or stepdaughter were around. "You hungry?" she asked. "We have another hour before close, but I already sent Keisha home. I'll probably close early and go upstairs to watch a movie with my family. I'm finishing up dinner for us now. There's plenty if you're hungry."

He was still overstuffed from the pizza, and there was plenty leftover in the mini fridge in his room. "No, I'm good. Thank you." He hesitated two seconds before rushing on. "So Keisha isn't here?"

Maggie paused her wiping. "No, the wind is getting terrible. I didn't want her on the road, and we were dead anyway."

Her choice of words made goose bumps crawl up his neck into his hairline, though he knew she meant nothing by it. The deaths he'd seen during his volunteer hours made it impossible now for him to use the word lightly. "Right."

What now? All the way downstairs, he'd been planning what he'd say to her. Now he felt let down. "Does she live with her aunt?"

"Goodness, no!" Maggie rolled her eyes. "She has her own place, of course." Her eyes narrowed. "Why?"

Obviously, she was leery of him after he'd upset Keisha this morning. "I need to talk to her."

"She'll be back tomorrow, and you can talk to her then." Maggie gave him a smile that was kind enough but still wary. During his stints in assisting doctors, he'd seen those looks often enough in the eyes of loved ones waiting to hear a verdict. He hated that Maggie now thought of him as some bad guy.

"Look," he said. "I think there's a misunderstanding. I didn't mean . . . I never meant to . . . What I need to say shouldn't upset her." He hoped. "Never mind." He turned to go back upstairs.

"Wait," Maggie said. "She lives on Third Street, on the north end. She has a cat mailbox. You can't miss it. But if it can wait, tomorrow is better." Her eyes drifted past him. "The storm's getting worse."

He looked outside, where it was now so dark it could be ten instead of six. "You're probably right. It'll wait."

Except by the time he was back upstairs, anxiety was gnawing in his gut. He still needed answers, both about his house and the past. Penny had said to talk to Keisha, so why not now during this storm when she couldn't be distracted by work?

Or run away from me, he thought with just a bit of a smirk. Of course, she could close the door in his face. Even so, he was going to do it. He *had* to do it, and he refused to stop to examine his motives further.

The café had another exit that led from the second floor near the rental rooms down to the parking lot, allowing boarders to come and go even when the café wasn't open. He had never used it since the café had always been open, but he decided to use it now so Maggie wouldn't hear him and give Keisha a warning.

He wanted this meeting to be unscripted. Yes, his initiating the confrontation gave him an unfair advantage, but he needed that where she was concerned. Otherwise, he ended up acting like an idiot.

Outside, the wind was strong in the parking lot, but the raw power of the storm sent a thrill through his body. Nature at its best—or worse. There was something primeval about it, and being outside all alone in the middle of the storm gave him a sense of adventure.

It took longer than expected to find Keisha's small house since she lived on the northern edge of town, not too far away from where she'd grown up. He was surprised to see her door standing wide open, the carpet of her front room poorly protected by the porch roof. As he hurried up the walk, lightning flashed, and mere seconds later, he heard the accompanying thunder.

Not good. Way too close. He took the three porch stairs in one leap and stuck his head inside the door, rapping loudly. "Keisha? You there? Your door's open."

No answer.

He called again, this time ringing the bell in rapid succession. An uneasy feeling rolled through his body, settling in his stomach. No answer and an open door could mean she'd gone outside for some reason, thinking she'd be right back but had been prevented from returning. Pivoting, he jumped down the stairs and headed around the back of her house. He'd reached her carport when he saw her kneeling next to a large row of bushes, her hands grabbing frantically at something inside the leaves. Or something was grabbing at her.

He hurried over. "Keisha, what are you doing? Do you know you left your door open?"

She turned to look at him, her head tilted awkwardly. "I

thought I shut the door . . . but what are you doing here? Ow!"
This last bit she said as she tried to tug free of the bush.

"Here, let me help."

He crouched next to her before she could refuse, grabbing
the branch and holding it steady as he untangled her hair. Even
above the rain, he could smell coconut coming from the wet
strands, and it brought back so many memories. He was glad for
the storm now because then she wouldn't see any stray emotion
coming from his traitorous eyes.

He finally freed her, but she grabbed the branches and pushed
it aside, putting her head at risk again. "What are you doing?"
he shouted above the rain. "You need to get inside. The lightning is close."

"I know." Her voice was nearly lost in the wind. "But my cat.
There's a leash . . ."

A cat and a leash? He'd never heard of such a thing. He parted
another section of bushes and then another. The end of a bright
pink leash caught his attention, and he reached for it, only to
have it disappear. He duck-walked further along the bush and
tried again. There. He dived for leash, feeling the sharp twigs
bite into his face. He came out triumphant, the end of the leash
in his hand. Keisha scooted toward him, reaching for the leash.
He tugged on it slightly but was afraid to pull too hard. Cats
were tiny creatures, and their necks didn't seem all that sturdy.

Keisha took the leash, and he parted the bush while she put
her head inside and steadily pulled out a white cat that wasn't a
kitten but still on the small side. It wore a halter, though, he saw
with relief, so not a lot of danger of strangling.

Keisha cuddled the stiff cat to her chest. The lightning flashed
again, and Xander's hair stood on end. It was at that moment he
saw the thing crawling on Keisha's skin—a gruesome and twisted

something heading up the leg of her shorts. Without thinking, he reached to brush it aside, but the moment his fingers touched scarred flesh, he knew what it was. This was no animal or wet garbage that she'd picked up in the brush, it was skin. Ravaged, broken skin, but alive nonetheless.

She pulled away, struggling with the cat, who howled with the thunder. "Better get inside!" she called. "Hurry!"

They ran to her door, which he'd shut to prevent more rain from blowing inside. Even so, the tile near the door was wet and slick.

Keisha leaned over and set the cat on the floor, releasing it from the halter. Immediately, it vanished through a doorway into what appeared to be a kitchen. Keisha stood and faced him, one of her hands in front of her right leg, where only a slice of the terrible scar was still showing. She didn't quite look him in the face.

What had happened to cause such a scar? His training told him it was no scratch from a bush or ordinary cut from a knife but something deep, terrible, and probably life-threatening. Her leg had been lacerated to the point of needing more than one skin graft, and it would have taken months to remove the bandage.

Someone in the know about her parents' deaths might assume she'd gotten the scar in the same fire that took their lives, but it wasn't a burn. She also had no scars when they'd dated, when she'd worn these same favorite shorts on any warm day, and even on a few cold ones. He remembered the shorts and also touching the smooth skin on her leg as if it had been yesterday.

"Want a towel?" she offered, keeping her eyes averted. If anyone needed a towel, she did. Her curly hair, blackened with rain, was wild and untamed, still trapping leaves and twigs from the bush. Mascara lined her beautiful hazel eyes and ran down her face while her shirt clung to every delicious curve.

He groaned mentally, and now it was him looking away. "Sure. Yes, please."

She left, still holding her hand in front of her leg as if hoping he hadn't seen her secret.

But he had, and his mind tumbled around the possibilities. Try as he might, he couldn't come up with anything that didn't involve some major accident.

When she returned minutes later, her hair was in some sort of tangled ponytail that was even more attractive than the perfectly straightened hair she'd worn in college because it left her long neck exposed. She'd changed her clothes as well to black pants and a sweatshirt, though she had to be sweating with the heat inside the house. He'd already shrugged off his jacket.

"Thanks," he took the towel and mopped his face and hair. The jacket had protected his shirt well enough, and the pants were only dampened. Still, he was back to feeling as if he were back in Washington DC during the muggy season.

She threw another towel on the tile and began stepping on it to mop up the water. Her bare feet left imprints on the towel as the water soaked through. Not a lot, after all, but enough to dampen the entire towel.

When she took back his towel, she handed him something else—a key.

"What's this?" He was genuinely puzzled because she was certainly not giving him a key to her house.

"It's to your grandfather's house. My aunt had the locks changed this morning after she heard you were in town. Apparently you're right, and I am the listed owner, so I give you permission to take anything you want from the house until you get it all sorted out."

Any vestiges of annoyance and anger bled from his heart.

Keisha hadn't lived an easy life, even if she'd been born with the proverbial silver spoon in her mouth, and he hated that he'd added to her hurt this morning by treating her as if she plotted his misery.

This show of faith meant he owed her an apology for this morning, and he'd grovel if he had to because this was the woman he remembered—the kind, thoughtful, and generous woman who had stolen his heart and breath with a single look. And despite her baggy shirt and messy ponytail, all he wanted at that moment was to take her in his arms and kiss her. Or even just hold her and tell her how much he'd missed being with her.

Yet something else burned a question in his soul. The scar— where had it come from? It called for investigation, as if searing through the black exercise pants she wore.

"Would you like some coffee or hot chocolate?" she asked, completely oblivious to his thoughts. "Or how about some food? I brought plenty of leftovers from the café." She gestured toward the takeout bags on a side table near the loveseat. "The rain might ease in a bit, but meanwhile you can dry out by the fire. I mean, I know it's hot in here already, but that should help your pants dry."

"I'd love coffee," he said. "I'm not really hungry, though, unless you have some butter cake."

She laughed. "I'm sure Maggie put some in. Have a seat, and I'll bring it in."

As she started toward the fireplace, he added, "Maybe while we sit, if you don't mind, you can tell me how you got the scar on your leg."

A swift intake of breath told him he'd surprised her. Her head shook once, violently. "No. I don't think so. In fact, it's getting late, and you already have what you want, so maybe you should leave right now in case the storm gets worse."

She was wrong. He didn't have what he wanted, and he hadn't since she'd left him in St. Louis. What's more, he wasn't going to leave here until she explained why she'd abandoned him, no matter how terrible it made him feel.

He'd be kind and gentle and make an effort to hold back accusations, but he had to know. It was time to put it behind him once and for all.

CHAPTER 12

Keisha's heart thundered in her chest. So he'd taken note of the scar when they were outside in the dark. She'd felt him brush her skin, though it was less sensitive there. However, she'd hoped she'd imagined it. But no, he'd seen the hideous scar, and now he wanted details. The gruesome details.

His head tilted while he studied her expression, as though trying to decide if she really meant for him to leave.

"I mean it," she said. "You should go."

"We don't have to talk about it then," he said, raising his hands in surrender. But something in his expression was set, and she couldn't quite trust that.

Without waiting for a response, he used first one toe and then another to take off his shoes before padding in stocking feet to the stuffed chair where she'd spent many winter nights curled up reading.

"This okay?" he said, settling into it with a sigh. "I'm not too wet, I don't think. I changed before I came. These are my step-father's clothes." Humor tinged his voice, and the moment to make him leave passed, mostly because she didn't want him to leave. It was good having him here. Familiar. Which was crazy. She'd have to take control of the conversation, the way she did at the café when men flirted with her. She was the queen of flirting while keeping men at arm's length. After all, harmless flirting increased tips almost as much as excellent service.

She flipped the switch on the gas fireplace before leaving to make coffee for him and hot chocolate for herself. She had no plans to spend all night—again—staring at the ceiling in a caffeine rush. She gave him his mug and a piece of butter cake before settling on the loveseat opposite him. It was sinfully comfortable and expensive, as all Olivia's furniture was, even the castoffs, and she couldn't help sighing just a little as she curled her feet up under her. The only thing missing was Cupcake, who would be off pouting somewhere until she was ready to make up.

"I turned down my thermostat so we don't boil," she said with a smile.

He sipped his drink. "You aren't having dinner? Or cake?"

She'd taken a few bites in the kitchen while waiting for the drinks to heat, enough to make the hunger leave, but her appetite had vanished. "I ate," she said shortly. She let a few seconds go by before continuing. "So, what will you take from your house?" She purposefully referred to it as his. Not only did she feel no connection to the house, but she liked the ease between them now. It felt strange and deliciously different from their other recent meetings. As long as he stayed away from personal questions.

"Well, maybe I won't need to take anything." He held the key out on the palm of his hand. "Since I plan to redeem the house, if possible. If that doesn't work out, I would like my grandpa's old cars, and my own . . . but there are other things. Even my mother wonders what we might have left behind. Now that she's older, it means more. I think back then when she left, she was anxious to get away, and then she had the twins, plus the diabetes is hard." He gave a slight snort. "Speaking of which, I'm apparently going to have another sibling. Tell me if that's not strange."

"You're so lucky." The words left her mouth before she could stop them. "I'd give anything to have a sibling. I have my cousin, though, so I guess that sort of counts."

He was tilting his head again, his gaze catching hers. "You lived with your aunt again after you came back to Forgotten?"

"For some months." She shrugged as if it had been no big deal even though every day for a year, she'd wished the ground would open up and swallow her. She'd raged at her dead parents, at him, at her aunt, and most of all, at herself. But then she finally pulled her life together and freed herself. Most of that was physical recovery, but a lot had been mental as well. She pulled up one knee and held it protectively to her chest as if doing so could ward off any further questions.

"About the house," he said. "I'm trying to get some cooperation with the city about the back taxes we owe, but your aunt could make it difficult."

She laughed. "My aunt makes everything difficult."

He smiled and nodded. "I can see that." His next words shocked her. "I've missed you, Keisha."

The admission shocked her because it hurt so much. He had no right to speak to her that way. Ignoring him, she gulped her hot chocolate, which had cooled to exactly the right temperature, and stared at the flames dancing around the faux log in the fireplace. She tasted nothing.

The next thing she knew, he'd set his mug on the coffee table and was sitting next to her. She inched away, masking her retreat with a glance at his mug. "Would you like more coffee?" But it was obvious his cup was still full.

"I'm good."

She was about to stand and put space between them when a streak of white zipped into the room and onto her lap. "Hey, sweetie," she crooned at the cat, who was obviously experiencing a little jealousy as she hissed softly at Xander.

"Okay, then," he said, grinning.

"She's just mad that we brought her in, even though she's scared of thunder." Keisha hugged the cat to her chest, her heartbeat steadying to its normal pace. The questions seemed to be over, and her outer emotions remained under control. "There's a mouse family that moved into the lilac bushes, and she insists on hunting them, though she's never really caught anything, or they probably would have moved by now."

"All claws and no teeth." He chuckled and reached out to scratch Cupcake's neck. The traitorous feline went boneless under his touch, and a purr started deep in her throat. Keisha could hardly blame her.

Wait, yes, she could. She pushed Cupcake toward him. There, with his hands busy, he'd forget about encroaching upon her space.

"So, you went to med school." She moved as far away from him as she could, though it wasn't much given that she was backed up against the arm of the loveseat. "How long had you been planning that?"

"Since leaving high school, I guess. It was always what I wanted, which is why I took all those chemistry classes."

"Ugh," she said, thinking of her online chemistry course.

"It's really not hard if you find it interesting."

Which was why she had to study overtime to get a passing grade. It wasn't that she couldn't understand it so much as she found so many other things more interesting, like painting her mailbox, scrubbing the oven, or even cleaning out the litter box.

"But after my third year of college," he continued, "I began to have doubts."

"So I guess that would be why you never mentioned it. Because you were changing your mind." She didn't buy it, not for a moment.

His nod was a little too quick. "Right. I wanted to do a few other things first or maybe something else instead of medicine."

"Africa like your grandfather." But she'd already half decided that had been a smoke screen to get money from her.

"Right." He fell silent, scratching the cat, who closed her eyes in bliss.

"But you would have already taken the exam to get into medical school," she pressed. "Why didn't you ever tell me?" She hadn't been a passing acquaintance, or at least it hadn't seemed that way at the time. Wouldn't he want input about his future from someone he supposedly loved? No, because he hadn't really loved her. He'd known about her inheritance, that was all. Tears stung her eyes, but she blinked them away quickly.

His hand stopped moving, and Cupcake, opening lazy eyes, patted him with a small paw. "Would it have made a difference?" Xander asked.

There were all kinds of innuendo behind the words. Her eyes narrowed. "What exactly are you implying?"

"I'm asking if knowing I'd been accepted to medical school would have made a difference with you. With your aunt."

Did he think that maybe her aunt would have approved of their marriage if she'd known? "What does my aunt have to do with any of it? You and I were close, or at least I thought so." She couldn't help the sting that entered her voice. "You should have at least mentioned it."

"I'd changed my mind about going, at least right then." His hand moved idly over the cat once more. "If you'd known, would it have changed things?"

He'd asked almost the same thing moments earlier, but now she saw a new meaning. "You mean would I have urged you not to go to Africa?"

His grin held no mirth, only sadness. "Something like that." He leaned over and set the cat on the carpet. Cupcake glared at him for a moment before lifting her tail proudly as if to prove her apathy at being abandoned. Then she stalked off with a plaintive meow to stand beside the front door.

"No, Cupcake," Keisha said. "You are not going outside."

"Also, with our backgrounds"—Xander leaned toward her as he spoke—"I didn't know if . . . I didn't want the fact that I'd been accepted to med school to be what impressed you."

He was too close, and her heart was doing those funny leaps again. She rose from the couch, trying to put space between them. If she didn't, she might not be able to keep herself from touching him.

"So you didn't want to impress me?" She smirked, meaning it to be a joke, to lighten the tension in the room again, because it was so thick she found it hard to keep her breath steady.

He stood gracefully to stand next to her. "Oh, I wanted more than anything to impress you." His voice had become low and husky again, an invitation her body screamed to accept. "But you have to admit that med school is something certain people care more about than anything else."

People like her aunt, he meant. But Keisha wasn't like her aunt, not then and not now, and she'd figure out how to explain that to him if only he wouldn't stand so close.

He didn't retreat, however, and the room around them fell away. In that moment, she was falling, falling toward him, seemingly without volition of her own. He caught her as he had on the roof. His strong arms and smell were still perfectly familiar even after all this time. She relaxed into him, and he groaned slightly, his hold on her tightening. The tension that had moments earlier threatened to tear them apart now pushed them together.

"I just wanted . . ." he began.

Whatever he was wanted was lost as thunder cracked outside, followed almost immediately by a flash of light. The next instant, they were plunged into darkness. She jumped away from him, relieved and also deeply disappointed.

"I hope that didn't hit the power plant," he said.

"Maybe not. It could be the wind knocking something over. I have flashlights."

But she couldn't find them in the kitchen, so she lit a few candles and was about to make her way back to him when he joined her. "I should go," he said. "It's getting bad out there."

"It's supposed to pass tonight, according to Fletcher Wilson, if you remember who he is."

"Jeremy's dad. Poor guy. I heard about his Alzheimer's."

"We could play cards, if you want. Wait it out." She was immediately sorry for the offer. Cards had been their go-to when they were bored in college. When other people watched movies or played video games, they played cards or board games. She still had her collection.

"Okay." He headed to her small, round table. "I admit I'm not looking forward to driving in that. Makes me remember the year my grandpa's truck was smashed by a falling tree."

Keisha shuddered, remembering the wind-borne brush that had been the cause of her own accident. Another driver had swerved to avoid it, angling into her path. With the poor visibility, she barely had time to note the oncoming car before slamming on her brakes and spinning out of control. They'd still collided. The other driver, a mature family man, had walked away unscathed. He'd come to see her during her two months in the hospital.

Unlike Xander.

She retrieved a deck of cards from a drawer, but her shiver hadn't gone unnoticed by Xander. "You used to love storms," he said, "but now they scare you."

She sat opposite him and shuffled the cards, loving the crisp way they fell perfectly into place. "They aren't fun to drive in, that's all." She kept her voice steady and was relieved when he didn't press. She hated that he seemed to know exactly how frightened she was of the storm.

While the tempest outside seemed to worsen, they played Kings in the Corner, Go Fish, War, Slap Jack, and several games of Speed, which she kept winning. "You were always good at this one," Xander said, laughing.

The comment sobered her instantly. Amazing how easily they had fallen into their old routine and how much she loved it. The candlelight cast a spell on her, one she recognized but didn't know how to change. Nostalgia prevented all negative thoughts.

They played on, with Cupcake sometimes rubbing against her leg and at other times settling on her lap, until finally she disappeared altogether, probably upstairs to her favorite spot at the foot of Keisha's bed. Keisha didn't miss her. She hadn't laughed so much in years. Four and a half years, to be exact.

"So what about you?" he asked as she set up yet another game. "Why did you decide not to go to law school?"

"I don't know. Things changed, I guess."

"You were having doubts in St. Louis. But every time I asked about it, you were so determined."

She did not remember that. Yes, she'd complained about the future attorneys in one of her classes, mocking their arrogance, but she hadn't realized her doubts started even before her accident. "I guess I really wanted to follow in my dad's footsteps. You know, to make him proud."

"I understand that because of my grandfather, but over the years, I've decided they'd really just want us to be happy with whatever we decide to do. And to be good, honest people."

That kind of thinking was what had given her the courage to admit she hated the idea of becoming an attorney. "Yeah, I think so."

She'd finished dealing, but Xander leaned back in his chair, watching her. "About your scar," he said.

She frowned and started to speak, but he lifted a hand and continued, "I said we didn't have to talk about it, but let me tell you what I know."

Her curiosity piqued despite her reluctance. "And what do you know?"

"I know it's an old wound, maybe two or three years old, and it was bad. Probably bad enough to land you in the hospital for quite a while. There would have been surgeries and grafts, and it likely hurt a lot. Am I right?"

Her insides felt wobbly. How could he know all that from a glimpse of her scar? *No, he'd touched it too,* she thought.

"Mostly," she conceded. Her stomach muscles clenched as she forced herself to speak lightly.

"What happened?"

"I was in a car accident."

He nodded. "That must have been the accident someone mentioned. I thought they were referring to the fire."

"It's no big deal," she lied, clenching her hands under the table. Obviously, it hadn't been a big deal for him. He'd taken money from Olivia and disappeared without so much as a goodbye.

"Still, coming across your friend like that yesterday couldn't have been easy." His voice was low, like a silky, sexy caress across her skin.

"I'm fine. She's fine. It all worked out."

He smiled ruefully. "I bet your case was a fascinating one for your doctors. For the wound to have left such a scar, there must have been severe damage. Still, with a good plastic surgeon, you could probably get a better result now."

The words stung. An entire year of pain and recovery all diluted to a simple sentence. "With a good plastic surgeon and a million dollars, you mean," she retorted. "Anyway, I don't care. It's not like anyone sees it, and it doesn't hurt." Which wasn't quite true. She did care, and sometimes it itched or stretched oddly.

"I'm really sorry," he said, dousing her indignation with his sincerity. "I didn't mean to . . . So when was the accident?"

She didn't respond. Instead, she set the cards down and went to the cupboard for a tall glass. No way was she going to tell him that an accident had been what kept her from returning to St. Louis. Better for him to believe she'd changed her mind about them rather than be cast in such a pathetic light—a woman injured and hospitalized, waiting for her faithless fiancé who never came.

"Would you like some water?" She'd already had two full cups of hot chocolate, and either the sugar or Xander's presence made her feel wired, so maybe she needed to avoid both.

"No, I'm fine."

She turned to find him standing right behind her. She drew in a swift breath.

"This has been good, hasn't it?" he said, an odd catch in his voice. Maybe he regretted dumping her, but it made no difference now, though truthfully, except for the plastic surgeon comment, it felt right being with him tonight. Fun. Thrilling. And she wasn't imagining the amazingly strong pull of attraction between them. If only . . .

No, she couldn't go there. Not after four and a half years. And certainly not after his comments about her scar. Yet he was standing so close, his eyes on her face and lips in a way that left no doubt as to what he was thinking. Maybe she should kiss him just once to prove to herself that it meant nothing and that her life was full without him. She could go on and live her own life and career, find love, and have a family. She didn't need him for anything.

Without considering any further, she lifted her face to his.

He reacted immediately, his lips angling over hers, his kiss greedy and demanding, startling her with its intensity. It was as if he'd been fighting the same battle all evening and had been waiting for this invitation—and maybe he had. Maybe this was why he'd remained at her house even after she'd given him the key. Perhaps he was as helpless as she was to prevent this moment.

Or maybe he was using her.

Again.

She pushed the thought away.

He tasted faintly of mint and heat. She arched toward him,

loving the strong feel of his body against hers. They had always fit so perfectly, and their bodies seemed to remember exactly what to do, even if a part of her mind felt so far out of depth that she might be drowning from bliss or fear or something without a name.

His kiss deepened, but instead of growing more demanding, it was slower now and more deliberate, as if gaining confidence. He explored her mouth, her cheeks, her neck, and the hollow behind her ear. His breath lifted her and made her as light as the cloud on which they floated together. She wanted to purr like Cupcake.

"What are we doing?" he murmured in her ear.

She didn't know, but she wanted to continue. Nothing else mattered, not the past or the future. Only this moment held any significance. Time was suspended and everything in her world was perfect.

Except the past *did* matter, and if she let him break her heart again, would there be any part of it left to ever find real love?

Suddenly coming to her senses, she pushed him away, her lips tingling where they'd touched his. He stared at her, his breathing heavy and deep. Then came a question she hadn't expected, "Why didn't you come back to me? What happened to change your mind? Or was that the plan all along? To leave me hanging?"

"What?" She stared at him blankly for long moments, her mind trying to understand the words. Finally, she shook her head. "I think the real question here is why didn't you look for me? Why didn't you talk to me instead of my aunt?" Because hitting her aunt up for money certainly didn't count as trying to make their relationship work.

Now it was his turn to stare, his eyes wide and dark with emotion. "I *did* look for you. I called your phone repeatedly.

You didn't answer. That should have been message enough, but I got in my car anyway and drove here to see you. Not that I could find you. It was like you'd dropped off the edge of the world."

The kitchen floor had oddly become uneven, and she was tripping and stumbling on unsteady, dangerous ground. "You looked for me?" The words felt like broken glass in her throat. This was the moment she'd been both dreaming of and dreading ever since she'd seen him yesterday morning. This was the confrontation where they demanded things of each other that were probably better left alone. A part of her always wanted to believe he'd looked for her, but the pragmatic part of her, the former budding attorney, knew it could never be.

Except here he was, claiming that he had come for her.

He flushed, clenching his hands at his sides. "Of course I looked for you. I was worried! I couldn't believe you would stay away, that you would give up all our plans." Hurt laced his voice, poorly concealed by his indignation. His hands unclenched, and he reached out as if to grab her shoulders, but instead, he shoved his hands into his pockets. "And you know what the worst thing is? You didn't even have the guts to face me and tell me yourself."

Of course guts had nothing to do with it. Tears pooled in her eyes, blurring his figure and making him seem further away. She was dizzy, like in the days after the accident when she'd awakened in the hospital. Yet she felt him close and could smell him like a memory she never wanted to let go.

Slowly, her vision cleared, and she found his eyes locked on hers. "Why wouldn't you see me?" he pressed. "Why did you leave it to your aunt to send me packing? Did I imagine St. Louis—us?" His voice was so tight, it nearly grated on her senses.

Words choked in her throat. She wanted to explain, to tell him everything. But doubt rose within her. He'd taken money from her aunt.

"Tell me," he growled. His voice was unyielding, his eyes unwavering. "I deserve that much. Anyone does."

Her words, when they came, surprised her. "It seems to me you went on just fine, Dr. Greenwood."

"No." His head swung back and forth. "I tried to. In a very real way, medicine saved me, but you were always my first choice."

"I don't believe that!" Because fate couldn't be so cruel to rip them apart that way, could it? "You didn't come for me."

"I tried!" His hands shot out, palms up in a pleading motion. "I swear I did! Ask your aunt."

"You mean the woman who gave you money to stay away?" she snarled, making her voice cold like Olivia's. "Then you didn't try hard enough. And now it's too late." She started toward the kitchen doorway. "Go back to the Butter Cake. Or stay, if you're afraid of the storm. But I'm going upstairs. We're finished here."

"But—"

"Please go."

His jaw worked, and for a moment, he looked as if he'd refuse, but then he nodded sharply. "Just now when I looked into your eyes . . . when you kissed me that way . . . I should have known. This is a game to you, isn't it?"

The words tore at her heart, ripping off the ragged bandage that had grown suffocating even while holding back a tsunami of sorrow.

She blinked and tears skidded down her cheeks. "You want to know when my car accident was?" Unbidden, her hand went to the hidden scar on her leg. "I'll tell you. It happened four and a half years ago on the night I was driving back to St. Louis. I was unconscious for days and in the hospital for two months. It wasn't a game, Xander. You just didn't try hard enough."

With that, she turned and walked into the darkness of the hallway, leaving him staring after her.

Xander watched Keisha leave, shock crashing over him. He'd been so proud of his medical knowledge and had not held back spouting off to Keisha, but he'd been wrong about her and wrong about the scar—by more than a year.

Tonight, he had had been determined to remind her of what they'd had lost and to demand answers. But all along she hadn't been at fault.

He had been.

Because with Keisha's parting words, his entire perception of the past shifted. She hadn't left him. She'd been unconscious in the hospital. No wonder she hadn't contacted him. Yes, her aunt had made it seem as if it had been her choice, but he should have insisted on seeing Keisha, on verifying her intentions. He should never have believed her aunt. He shouldn't have taken the woman's money, either, even if he had accepted mostly out of spite to show Keisha that he wouldn't simply stop living without her. He had a sneaking suspicion that one of the reasons he'd made it through the grueling years of medical school was because he'd wanted to prove something to her.

None of this, however, was what rooted him to the spot. No, it was the fact that she'd been lying in a hospital bed alone when she'd needed him most. He should have been there with her, holding her hand and telling her it was going to be okay. Instead, he'd let her down in a life-altering way. How could he ever expect her forgiveness? No wonder she didn't trust him. Ignorance and youth meant nothing in this instance. He'd been fighting for what he wanted all his life, ignoring all those who doubted him, but he'd let the most important thing slip from his fingers.

All my fault.

Something rubbed against his leg, and he looked down to see the white cat there, her green eyes catching the dim light of the candles and reflecting it back to him.

"Should I go after her?" he asked.

The cat only meowed mournfully. His feelings exactly.

By not fighting for his relationship with Keisha four years ago, he'd thrown everything away. Everything he'd dreamed of. He might not be a doctor now if they hadn't broken up, but they could be in Africa together, helping others, or they might have returned to the States to start a family. Maybe he'd only now be starting med school.

He'd slog through it all again if it meant having her beside him.

He went to the front door and stared out at the storm. It seemed to be lessening in intensity, but he wasn't leaving Forgotten or even Keisha's house. He'd left too soon once before. If there was even the slightest chance for them, it was now or never.

Was it possible to make up for the hurtful years apart? They were different people now, changed by their separate experiences, and it was possible they'd lost the special something that would make the difference in the long run.

Except he didn't believe that because every time he saw her, his heart jumped and yearned and reached out for what might have been.

The only thing he could do was try. He was his grandfather's child, and he would not give up until she ordered him to go.

CHAPTER 13

Keisha awoke to the sound of nothing. No storm, no rain. It was over. She smiled, thinking about old Fletcher Wilson. Then she remembered last night.

The kiss.

The confession.

The eyes swollen with tears.

She had lost him again . . . because that's what it felt like. What's more, this pain was her own fault. She'd made a mistake letting him in last night. If he had taken the key and gone, there would have been no easy card games that evoked good memories or a kiss that made the few kisses she'd shared with other men pale in comparison.

But he'd looked for her. She felt the ring of truth there.

Maybe.

Her mind replayed the kiss.

What did he think of her now that he knew? That she was

pathetic? That she was waiting for an apology? That maybe he still had a shot at her inheritance?

No, he was a doctor now, and any monetary lack was temporary.

In the end, nothing had changed, because no matter how the past had played out, he hadn't found her four years ago. He hadn't given her a chance to explain. He'd taken Olivia's money and agreed not to contact her. Though, thinking about it, she hadn't contacted him either after believing he dumped her. If she had called, would everything be different?

She sighed heavily before grabbing her cell phone to check her messages, but it was completely out of battery, so she plugged it in. Nothing happened. Of course. Just her luck that the electricity was still off. She left the phone and rolled from the bed.

Something in the air, previously wafting out of conscious thought, caught her attention. Was that . . . food? It smelled delicious, like the Butter Cake every morning except here in her own house. But Maggie would be at the café now, her generator hard at work so she could keep cooking for the town. More likely, it was her uncle, Josiah, who had a key he'd promised never to share with Olivia. Her uncle was a decent cook when he took the time, even better than Olivia.

Keisha felt a lessening of the grip around her heart at the thought of being with a kindred soul. She was glad Josiah would be in Forgotten long after his divorce and Olivia's departure. He had filled the role left by her missing father much more completely than Olivia had been able to fill her mother's shoes.

Pulling on the decidedly dirty pink T-shirt from the night before and her too-short shorts that had dried overnight in the heat of the house, she hurried to the bathroom to splash water on her face. The swelling of her eyes from last night had nearly disappeared, and her uncle should think nothing of it. He wouldn't mind the scar on her leg, either, or ask about it, as he'd seen it before and was aware of her sensitivity about it.

Was Xander already on his way back to Panna Creek with his antique cars? Thinking of him brought heat to her face, and she splashed more water on her skin until it felt cooler. As she patted it dry, Cupcake streaked into the room, rubbing against her legs and begging to be petted.

"I'll get you food in a minute," she said. "But where were you this morning, you little traitor? Why didn't you wake me?" The smell of the food must have enticed her away.

Before going downstairs, Keisha gathered a basket of dirty clothes to wash before work. She had practically nothing clean left in her closet. Tomorrow, they'd close early, but today, they'd be busy at the café, making more gooey butter cakes for the festival. Meanwhile, her house was somehow hotter than it had been last night.

She had the laundry in the machine before she realized it wouldn't work without electricity. "Some pioneer you'd make," she muttered with a laugh. Well, she'd leave it on, and it would start when the power went on. She'd zip home on her break to put the load in the dryer.

With Cupcake in her arms, she finally headed into the kitchen, her mouth watering in anticipation. "Why aren't you at town ha—" The words died on her lips when she saw Xander cooking over a camp stove.

"Hi," he said, turning to grin at her as if her confession last night had never happened. "I hope you like pancakes and bacon and eggs because it's pretty much the only breakfast I know how to make. Well, besides a truly awful egg casserole that my mother taught me to make. My roommates in med school wouldn't even eat it, and that's saying a lot."

She laughed at his expression and the way his hair was standing up in the back, as if he'd slept on it all wrong. Maybe she should be angry seeing him still here, but her betraying heart began thumping with excitement.

"Did you sleep on my loveseat?"

"If you can call what I did on that uncomfortable piece of furniture sleeping, then yes."

"Hey, watch it. It's perfectly comfortable."

"Not if you're six feet tall." He deftly turned the pancake on the camp stove. "And who did the painting on this wall? That yellow is seriously bright. Guess I didn't notice last night in the dark."

"It's a work in progress," Keisha had wanted cheerful walls, but the color turned out rather garish, so she'd only finished two-thirds of the room. "Anyway, where'd you get the camp stove? I'm pretty sure I don't own one."

"Well, since I have the key, I went back to my grandpa's and snagged his, except it was in the workshop out back, and I had to get inside through the window—which reminds me, there's water damage there too I'll need to fix, so if you could find out the combination to the lock, it would be helpful."

"Sure, okay." She sat down on a chair, mostly because her knees were wobbly, but then realized that sitting pulled the shorts up and exposed more of her hideous scar. She put her hand over it and looked up quickly to find him watching her. Mortified, she felt completely undressed, as if he were staring at the most private part of her.

"I'm so sorry you went through that," he said, moving toward her. "I should have been there with you."

"You should have." It was good to hear him acknowledge it, even if it possibly meant she'd been wrong about him all these years.

"I also know I have a lot more to make up for." The spatula clattered to the ground when he dropped it and swiftly knelt in front of her, his eyes locked on hers. "Are you willing to give me another chance? I know we're both different now, but I think last night proved we still have something, or could. If we wanted."

He fell silent, watching her. More words hung between them, unsaid. Did she want them said? She was distinctly aware of him waiting for some response. She felt a rush of desire, an urge to reach out and touch his face, rough with day-old beard. She longed to run her fingers through his hair and explore all the curves and edges of him. Yet, at the same time, her thoughts tumbled, and she found it hard to catch a breath.

"Keisha?" Xander's worried voice came from far away. "Are you okay? Because you look like you might faint."

That was it exactly. She was light-headed and dizzy with a panic attack, like those she'd experience after her parents' deaths and then again after her accident. But this wasn't the same. She wasn't losing anyone, not even Xander—he'd already been lost.

Unless she was worried about losing him again, which might be even worse.

He took her hands. "Breathe, Keisha. In and out. Do it with me."

She followed his prompting, and the panic receded. Breathing actually helped. Go figure. But his question remained unanswered. What was her response? She opened her mouth to say something, unsure of what might come out, but she was interrupted by the faint ringing of her doorbell.

His eyes strayed from her face to the kitchen doorway and then back again. "What do you say?"

"No kissing," she said.

"What?" He blinked in confusion.

"I believe in second chances." She always had, which was one of the reasons she'd been interested in becoming an attorney all those years ago, to help those who might have gone astray. "But no kissing until I'm sure."

He arched one brow, a smile tugging at the corners of his mouth, dimpling his cheeks in a most fascinating way. "Are you sure? Because that seems to be something we still do really well."

He was right, but being physical with him wouldn't take care of her trust issues. No, she needed to keep him at arm's length and her head on straight. She frowned, and he nodded.

"Okay, deal. I get it. You need to trust me again, and I can live with that. But I'm not going anywhere this time, I promise."

Technically, she'd been the one to leave, but the extenuating circumstances made much of the fault his. "Not even to Africa?"

"Maybe after residency, if I make it work. It's still there waiting with plenty to do." His smile was so gentle, it made her heart ache. This was the man she'd fallen for. Both this and the sexy, passionate man she'd kissed last night, but she wouldn't let herself think about that.

A pounding on her kitchen door startled them both. She jumped up and hurried to open it before considering that it might be Olivia, who wouldn't be happy to find Xander here making her breakfast. Too late—Keisha had already begun opening the door.

"Oh, hi, Laina!" Keisha blinked in surprise to see Laina standing on the top stair that led into the kitchen from her carport area. Her arm was in a sling and her foot in a boot, but her makeup was as heavy as usual, her frizzy hair tamed into a French braid.

"Sorry to barge in, but there's been an emergency." She hesitated when her gaze went past Keisha to Xander, who was once again flipping pancakes. "Oh, hi," she said. "I didn't see you there."

Keisha opened her mouth to say it wasn't what it might look like but then shook off the urge. She didn't need to explain.

"Nice to see you on your feet," Xander said with a grin that showed his dimple to its best advantage. "Would you like some breakfast?"

Laina shook her head. "I've already eaten. My mother has been taking really good care of me—a little too good, if you get my drift." She gave a longsuffering sigh as she hobbled past Keisha without invitation and dropped into a chair near the table. "She hasn't let me out of her sight since the accident, and she is quite upset that I left without her this morning. But since she and Ronica are good friends, she didn't have a choice after what happened this morning."

Pushing the door shut, Keisha went to sat opposite Laina at the table. "Wait, is that the emergency? Did something happen to Ronica Wilson?"

"No, not her. Her husband. They've taken him to the hospital in Panna Creek. They don't know if he's going to make it."

"Oh, no!" Keisha blinked back sudden tears. She hadn't known Fletcher well when he was all right in his head, but she'd come to know the new him, and Ronica as well, during her years at the café. The Butter Cake was Fletcher's favorite place to eat breakfast and read the newspaper he could no longer understand. In his moments of lucidity, he was kind and often humorous, while in his unknowing moments, he was lost and young, his hair sticking up like an aged little boy just come from his bed. Only a few times had he become petulant, and Maggie usually could soothe him with heavily buttered cinnamon toast.

"I know, right?" Laina tucked a stray lock of frizz behind

her ear. "Ronica woke up early this morning, and Fletcher was missing—again. Somehow, he undid the locks she has on the doors, so they started looking. Jeremy found him out in their alfalfa field, lying there as peaceful as could be on crushed alfalfa stalks, like he was in bed, staring up at the sky. Ronica told my mom he looked comfortable. I mean, the alfalfa was damp, and the ground underneath soaked, but since no one cuts alfalfa in September, there was enough to make a sort of barrier, I guess. And even this early, it's getting really hot out there, exactly like Fletcher predicted."

"Is he conscious?" Xander asked.

"He wasn't responsive when they found him, but Doc treated him for shock while they waited for the ambulance from Panna Creek, and he said Fletcher was stable when they took him. Because of the rain, it took a long time for the ambulance to get here, though the road should be clear by afternoon with this heat." Laina sighed. "Ronica went on for quite some time about how she would make the town council pay for drainage on the road. In fact, she asked me to put up a donation box during the festival, and she's sending out an email."

"Poor Ronica," Keisha said. "Jeremy told me he always finds his father out in the fields when he gets away from whoever's watching him. Guess that's where he loved to be the most. With his mind going . . . well, Fletcher once told me he hoped the end would be fast. For Ronica's sake, I mean. Maybe he'll get his wish."

Laina nodded. "Maybe, but it's still sad. He's so young. Not much older than my father. And Ronica's distressed about losing him, as you can imagine." Laina gave her head a shake and stiffened her back. "But she's insisting that the Harvest Festival will go on as planned. That's why I'm here. The Ladies Auxiliary is taking over Ronica's duties for the Harvest Festival. Ronica made a list, but we couldn't reach you, so I volunteered to come over."

It was like Ronica to think of the town even while her husband was fighting for his life. "Sorry, my cell phone's dead," Keisha told Laina.

"Same for a lot of the younger members of the Auxiliary, and many of the older women's home phones don't work without electricity. Guess there is something to be said for those old corded phones that have the handset plugged directly into the base. My mom's still works fine."

"I think I saw one of those antiques at my grandpa's house this morning," Xander said. "I could go get it if we need to." He winked at Keisha, which sent a flutter of butterflies through her stomach. Or were they wasps about ready to sting?

Laina laughed. "You might have to. Or hit me up for a charged battery. My dad has enough backup charging devices that our whole family could probably do without electricity for a week. Shouldn't be necessary, though. They'll get it back up." She laid a paper on the table Keisha hadn't noticed in her hand before. "Ronica's responsibility list is way longer than those she assigns out to each of us, but I've divided it up, and it's doable. I'm giving you and Olivia all of Ronica's activity booths. There were apparently four that she didn't delegate to anyone else. Details are on this paper. Just make sure all the booths get set up and the volunteers know when they're supposed to be there. I don't know exactly how far Ronica went on all the prep, but she always believed the festival was going to happen, so it's probably not going to be too intensive. I thought you'd prefer activities over the food. I gave those to Maggie since she's already doing her butter cake and bread."

"Thanks, I do prefer them."

Laina frowned as she stood and moved back to the door. "You'll talk to Olivia about working on the booths with you, right? She hates me, and I'd probably do something stupid, like ask her why the town council didn't approve drainage on the road already."

"That would be dangerous," Keisha agreed, hurrying after Laina so she could open the door for her. Her aunt hated to be wrong. Better to make her think it was her own idea, a difficult endeavor without getting caught. Her uncle had once been a master at that, but somewhere along the line, he stopped trying so hard. And who could blame him?

"If Olivia hates you, you're in good company." Xander turned off the camp stove and joined them. "Hate is probably a mild word compared to what she thinks of me." His voice was light, but his veiled glance at Keisha held no mirth.

Laina giggled a little too forcefully, as if Xander made her nervous, or as if she liked him, and Keisha experienced a tiny rush of irritation before she could stop herself. Giving Xander another chance didn't mean he was already hers.

"Well, I'd better get going. I have a few other lists to pass out." Laina's eyes rested on Xander's face. "But I'm glad you're here because I wanted to thank you for what you did for me yesterday." Her gaze widened to include Keisha. "For what you both did for me yesterday."

"We're just glad you're okay." Xander put an arm around Keisha, his hand resting heavily on her opposite shoulder as though it were something he did all the time. He cast Keisha a mischievous grin that dared her to pull away.

Instead, she put her hand over his, patting it with exaggeration. "Yes, we are. And since Xander is still in town dealing with his house, I guess I should put him to work." She grinned at him, batting her lashes twice for emphasis. "You'll do an hour at the dunking booth, right? That's two shifts. I've scheduled them in half-hour increments to work around other booth volunteers."

"Only if you'll do a shift as well," he returned.

"Actually, I can't since I'll have to make sure Ronica's other booths are functioning. I can't do that wet."

His brow raised. "Why not? It's hot outside now, and you might thank me. Besides, you might not get wet, depending on how good of an aim your enemies have."

Laina giggled again. "Or friends. Last year Jeremy Wilson spent a whole wad of cash trying to dunk her. If she got up there again, he'd never let her down before it happened."

"Oh, really. I guess I'll have to have a chat with him." Xander's laugh sounded strained, though Keisha doubted anyone else would be able to tell. Or was that wishful thinking?

Laina laughed with him, punching Keisha lightly with her good hand. "I think you've been holding out on me, girl. But you two look good together. When there's more time, I want the whole story of how you two met."

"Uh, sure," Keisha said, trying to keep a straight face. That wasn't going to happen, of course, unless . . . what if Xander was for real? Would her broken heart heal, or did the scarring go too deep? Trusting him again seemed impossible, but if he was telling the truth about everything, maybe she was every bit as much at fault.

I have to talk to Olivia, she thought. Because somehow everything started and ended with her aunt. Josiah might also know some of what had been going on, but his marriage to Olivia was already in trouble long before Keisha's accident, so it was possible he hadn't been an active party to what Olivia had done.

"I'll start on this right away," Keisha said, pulling away from

Xander and the heat that threatened to make her brain stop working. Her eyes darted to the cat clock on the wall above her table. "Speaking of which, I'd better start on this list if I'm going to finish before I have to work. I mean, I can do some from there, but . . ."

"I can help," Xander said, taking the paper from her hand. "If there's one thing I learned in med school, it's how to organize." He patted his pocket. "And my phone still has a charge."

"Show off!" Keisha rolled her eyes, and his grin widened like in the old days. It felt so good.

"Med school?" Laina looked impressed. "I didn't know you were a doctor."

"Guilty as charged."

That was apparently Laina's cue to let her eyes dip openly to Keisha's scar, curiosity written on her face. "Is that what happened in the car accident?"

Keisha's breath caught again in her throat. Silly when it was, after all, just a scar. The mark of a survivor. A badge of honor since it meant she'd survived.

"Yes," Xander answered for her. "It's awesome, but you'll have to talk about that later." He glanced at Keisha. "Better eat fast while the food is still warm. You can change after. Don't wear a jacket, though. When I said it was hot, I meant it. It's like we're back in August or something."

"He's right." Laina stepped through the doorway onto the top stair leading into the carport. "Oh, and I almost forgot. Ronica wants us to remind everyone we see today to set out their harvest donations on Main Street or bring them to the festival."

"Okay," Keisha said. "I'll stop by city hall and ask my uncle to send out an email."

Laina nodded. "Good idea, but he's probably already done it.

He was out at the Wilson farm with Doc and Ronica, waiting for the ambulance."

"I'm not surprised. He and Ronica are good friends. She's been in charge of most of the festivals for the past . . . well, ever since I can remember." Keisha had only begun paying attention after starting work at the Butter Cake and joining the Ladies Auxiliary.

"Right. How your uncle is so nice when your aunt. . ." Laina shook her head and left the sentence dangling with a little wave.

Keisha closed the door and took the list back from Xander, frowning.

"Doesn't look too bad," Xander said, stepping closer. "I don't know anything about face painting, but the soda toss and woodworking notes say all the supplies are at town hall, and there is a list of volunteers to call for a reminder. I'll just snap a picture and take care of those for you." He pulled out his phone.

"That would help a lot, but I'm more worried about the kissing booth. I said it was a bad idea when we were all planning the festival, but it looks like Ronica decided to do it anyway."

"That wouldn't take much preparation, right?" He laughed. "Maybe a box of breath mints and a bunch of eager high schoolers?"

She couldn't help the slight snort that escaped her lips. "I guess. Ronica did say it was one of the best moneymakers last year."

"I can understand that. Especially if the girls were pretty." Xander winked.

"Women *and* men," Keisha corrected. "And only quick pecks are permitted, mostly on the cheek."

He shrugged. "Either way, a kissing booth could only work in a small town like this. In the big city someone would turn it into a political fight. And at least here you know almost everyone. Who to avoid and the like."

"There is that." She'd made the mistake of volunteering for the booth two years ago, and it had mostly been kissing grizzled old farmers or schoolboys on the cheek while onlookers laughed good-naturedly. Well, there had been a cute attorney she'd been teased into kissing on the mouth, but there hadn't been any kind of connection between them, and when he asked her out later, she thanked him but declined.

"Even if I knew any high school girls here," Xander said, "I wouldn't touch a kissing booth with a ten-foot pole. I read all the sexual harassment literature in med school, and for a man, it's a lawsuit waiting to happen."

Keisha laughed out loud this time. She'd forgotten how much he made her do that. "Even in a small town?"

"Yes." He forked a couple of pancakes onto a plate that already contained bacon and eggs. "Tell you what, if you end up having to volunteer, I'll buy up all your kisses."

"I said no kissing."

He pushed the food into her hands. "Okay, whatever you want." His gaze held hers. "That is still what you want, right?"

At that moment, she wanted only to step into his arms and try out a few kisses, or, at the very least, trace his dimple with her finger. "Yes, and you agreed."

"Okay then. Just checking. I'll be sure to send the old-timers and eager boys your way."

She rolled her eyes. "Good to know I can count on you."

His face sobered. "You can, Keisha. I promise."

She didn't know that, not for sure, but she'd wait and see. She began to eat, feeling his eyes on her face.

And she loved it.

CHAPTER 14

Full of pancakes, eggs, and bacon, Keisha locked her door and headed for her car. She'd found an old skirt she never wore in the very back of her closet to change into and a white work blouse from the dirty clothes in the washer that didn't smell too bad. She'd pass muster at work, she hoped.

First, she had to give the face painting booth duties to Olivia. Her aunt would never deign to run the kissing booth, but she did have some artistic skills, so as long as Keisha framed it correctly, the face painting would be something she might agree to oversee. Olivia would probably end up overdoing it and scare away half the volunteers, but she'd find new ones, and the kids would be happy with whatever she did.

She beeped the car to unlock it, and Xander reached to open the door. "Thanks for letting me crash on your couch."

"Thanks for breakfast." How had his face become so familiar again in such a short time? It was as if her soul had never forgotten him.

"You sure you don't want to use my phone?"

"No, mine will charge some in the car on my way to my aunt's house. And Maggie has a generator with an adapter at the café. Besides, you'll need yours to call the volunteers for your booth. It'll be easier than Maggie's landline."

His eyes slowly traced her lips. "Well, if you're sure."

He meant both about the not-kissing and the phone—the double entendre wasn't lost on her. The sexual tension between them was both exhilarating and terrifying. She didn't understand how that could be when the world around them seemed so normal now that the rain had ceased. She was teetering on top of the world, exalted and free, a feeling that was as familiar as each contour of his face.

He turned as if to start down the drive to his car but hesitated before saying, "While you're at your aunt's, would you mind asking her about the back taxes on my house? If the town council agreed to waive the fees, it would help a lot. They're more than the taxes themselves. I mean, I could defer my school loans and work something out with my bank, but that doesn't stop the interest from accruing, so I'm reluctant."

"That's right. You mentioned my aunt was making things difficult."

"Well, I only assumed it was her since . . ." He shrugged, looking adorably uncomfortable. "But yeah, I think she might have it out for me."

"I'll talk to her." An odd sensation twisted in her gut, though she couldn't pinpoint why. Maybe it was the idea of confronting Olivia.

"Thanks."

She climbed in her car and drove away, watching him stare after her in her rearview mirror.

Her heart was singing. Xander was back, and maybe this time . . .

She couldn't bear finishing the thought. If she began hoping, would the letdown be as bad as before? No, she wouldn't let herself go that far. She'd keep the most tender part of her protected, the part next to the pain of losing her parents. *That's it. I can take him or leave him.*

But already, she wasn't quite sure that was true.

Her aunt was home in her pristine kitchen, wearing a flowing, cream-colored dressing gown that was fancy enough to be worn to a cocktail party but was, in fact, bedroom loungewear. The white contrasted with her ebony skin and upswept, braided hair that was one of her more elaborate wigs. Obviously, she planned to go out soon.

"Darling, what a pleasant surprise," Olivia said as if they hadn't argued the day before. Her gaze dropped to Keisha's skirt and blouse, and while she didn't comment on the choice or the wrinkles, Keisha felt her judgment. "And you're just the person I was going to call. I trust you received the key I had the locksmith leave at your house yesterday and that it wasn't lost with all the wind and rains last night."

"I found it. Thanks." Not in a million years would she admit she'd already given it to Xander. In case Olivia asked, it was better to get straight to the point of her visit. "Have you heard about Fletcher?" Keisha asked.

Olivia nodded. "Yes. A sad state of affairs, but it's really for the best. He's been only partially there for what? Maybe four years now? And Ronica is still young enough to live another life."

Keisha was offended on the Wilsons' behalf. "She *loves* Fletcher and takes wonderful care of him. And why do I feel you're talking more about yourself than Ronica?"

Olivia chuckled. "Touché. So what brings you here? With that ghastly rain finally gone, I'm on my way into town, but I have time for a cup of coffee if you'd like one."

"No, thanks. I had a big breakfast. I couldn't drink another drop." A smile tugged on Keisha's lips as she remembered Xander in her kitchen. "I just stopped by to give you another assignment. We're all taking over Ronica's jobs for the Harvest Festival. Many hands make light work and all that."

"I'm already overseeing the food donations and distribution," Olivia arched her neck a little proudly. The food for the poor was the most important tradition of the Harvest Festival, after all. Ronica had assigned it to Olivia for the past two years, mostly because it was the only thing she didn't complain about.

"I know, and it's a lot of work." Or at least it was work for Olivia's fellow town council members who were always at her beck and call. "But this is right up your alley." She gave her Laina's list. "A face painting booth. You and I were actually assigned all four of these other booths, but I've got those in hand, and they're all kind of silly. The face painting booth is artistic and very popular with the kids, though, so I thought you would be fantastic at it. I'd run it myself, but you know me and paint."

"I've seen your kitchen walls," Olivia responded dryly. She pulled out a pair of readers from a breast pocket and stared at the paper.

Keisha rushed on. "I'm impressed with everything Ronica does. I mean, I only had the dunking booth to run, and she had four other activity booths plus more they're assigning out. She must be a bit of a perfectionist to keep so much for herself. I know it's her job, but I also know the city pays her next to nothing."

Olivia's gaze lifted from the paper. "She's trying to escape by throwing herself into work. Can't blame her, given what she's going through with Fletcher."

That made a strange kind of sense, but again Keisha felt Olivia was also talking about herself. "I guess. Poor Ronica."

"Very well," Olivia said, her voice becoming businesslike. "I suppose there is still time enough to salvage the booth. Hold on while I make a copy." She disappeared through a doorway, heading in the direction of the office that had once been Josiah's. Had he moved his stuff out already, or was he waiting until Olivia left town to come back and take up where he'd left off?

When Olivia returned, Keisha stuffed the paper in her purse as her aunt said, "Don't forget you're helping with the food collection on Main Street. We can't have the horses and wagons stopping traffic for long. You know the songs, don't you?"

Keisha had been singing the Forgotten Harvest Festival songs since she was a child. "Of course I know the songs, and don't worry. I'll be wearing the same pioneer costume as last year."

"Okay then." Olivia took a deep breath. "Now, if there's nothing more, I need to dress."

Keisha took a breath. "There's one more thing."

"Oh?" Her aunt smoothed the material of her dressing gown near her hip, as if rubbing at an invisible stain.

"I'd like you to urge the council to drop the non-payment fees on Xander's house."

The slightest gasp escaped Olivia's reddened lips. "But that means the city will lose money it can't afford to lose. And so will we."

"The city will also benefit from a new taxpayer." Did she dare hope that Xander might stay? "And the city will give us back our money from the sale."

Olivia stiffened. "You're not so rich that you can pass up

investment opportunities. Now's the time to make the best movements since you're young and can take risks. Plus, we'll lose all the time that we haven't used the money for something else."

Keisha sought the words that might move her aunt. "Money isn't more important than people. My dad taught me that. It's Xander's grandfather's house, and he wants it."

"He wants it today, but he's only going to sell it and make the money we would have made."

"As he should." Why couldn't her aunt see that? "Look, I want him to be happy."

"Don't tell me." Disdain dripped from Olivia's voice as she stared at Keisha with narrowed eyes. "Is this to get him back?"

Keisha thought of Xander kneeling in front of her in the kitchen that morning, his wonderful eyes pleading. "No, but I don't wish him ill. It's what I would do for anyone. Taking someone's house against their will is not who I am. Please, Olivia." Keisha couldn't say more. The words welled up in her throat and wouldn't come out. All she could do was to repeat, "Please."

Olivia closed the space between them. "Did he put you up to this? Did he ask you to make this request?"

Keisha couldn't help thinking about Xander's words in her carport. He had asked, but that didn't mean anything, did it?

When Keisha didn't respond right away, Olivia added, "Because something tells me it is."

Keisha ignored the comment. "And while you're talking to the council, you really need to approve funds for the road drainage. Laina might have needed to go to the hospital, and Fletcher had to wait hours for the ambulance to come by the long route." Oops, there she went, stepping into the road confrontation Laina had so wanted to avoid, but now that she'd already annoyed her aunt, what was a little more? Especially if it took Olivia's mind off her hatred for Xander for a few moments. "Our community needs the road to Panna Creek, and the council has to figure out a way to make it happen."

"Believe me," Olivia retorted, "if there were funds, we'd have approved it already."

"Well, I'm designating all the proceeds from the booths I'm overseeing to a road fund."

"You can't do that. It's for the poor."

Keisha huffed in exasperation. "And the poor need a road and an ambulance they can count on!" The darkening of Olivia's face told her the comment would put her on the naughty list for months to come.

Good, she thought. *Maybe she'll actually do something.* Immediately, she knew she should feel bad for having the thought, but she didn't. Not one little bit.

"What Forgotten needs is a hospital," Olivia said. "That's one of the reasons I've urged Charlie to become a doctor, though it hardly matters now that I'll be leaving after he graduates. I'm hoping he'll choose to live nearer civilization."

Charlie loved Forgotten and would never become a doctor. How could her aunt not see either of those things? "Seems to me you and the council already have a chance at enticing another doctor to stay in town." Her aunt seemed as blind to that possibility as she was to her son's dreams.

Olivia's nostrils flared, a sure sign of anger. "You need to be careful around Xander Greenwood. He's not one of us."

"One of us?" Keisha stared at her. "Do you mean those who have money? Because I'm pretty sure in the next year or two, he'll earn more than I have in my entire life. Or do you mean our color? Because almost no one else in Forgotten is either." Strange that the only prejudice she'd ever felt had come from her

aunt, who didn't have "tainted" white genes like Keisha and her
parents. "Or do you mean he's not from Forgotten? Because he
can trace his family nearly all the way back to the founding of
the town, which was long before my parents moved here."

"You know what I mean."

Keisha didn't. "I have to go to work." She turned and started
for the door, though there was more she wanted to know.
Specifically, she wanted to know what happened between Olivia
and Xander when he'd come looking for her in Forgotten. But
she didn't have time now for this confrontation. "I'm going to be
pressed as it is to call all the volunteers for my booths."

Olivia hurried after her, lips pursed, but she said nothing.
Keisha practically ran to her car, relieved when Olivia stayed at
the door to her very large and beautiful home, the one she would
abandon the instant Charlie left for college.

Keisha couldn't tell if she was running from Olivia to avoid
further confrontation or because she was afraid of what more
she might learn about Xander. Did it mean she was beginning
to trust him again? Or that somewhere deep inside she knew he
wasn't trustworthy?

Olivia watched her niece drive away, a sinking feeling in her
stomach. Why couldn't the girl see what was so clear to her?
Xander Greenwood had ruined Keisha's life once, but Olivia
wouldn't let him do it again. She owed it to her brother, who
had entrusted her with his daughter's future, to find a way to
show Keisha Xander's true color, which had nothing to do with
his skin. So what if he had made it through medical school? The
way he was using Keisha to do his dirty work with his house fees
proved he was still trash. Olivia had to protect Keisha. But how?

Then, she knew. Once a rat, always a rat. And she had just the right cheese.

With a tight smile, she went back into the house to change.

Keisha couldn't believe how busy the Butter Cake was when she arrived. Or how hot. Maggie needed to reserve the generator's power for cooking only, so the doors were propped open to catch any stray breeze, though it didn't seem to be working.

"I hope they get the power back on quickly," Maggie said, tossing her a yellow apron as she walked into the kitchen.

"No one seems to mind." Already, Keisha was sweating. She put on the apron and twisted her hair up.

Maggie grinned. "They're all excited about the Harvest Festival. Half of them believe the ghost of Chelsea Morgan changed the weather. It's so hot that some doubt we'll need to lay boards under the booths. The fairgrounds have great drainage."

"Better put them down anyway. There's been a lot of rain."

"That's what I said." Maggie reached for the switch on her bread mixer. "Laina and her many siblings are getting that done as we speak. To her mother's dismay, of course. She wants Laina in bed."

Keisha smiled, picturing a hammer-wielding Laina. "She always was the first one to jump into anything when we were kids. Strange how I didn't remember that until just now."

"Well, you've been busy." Maggie hesitated before adding, "How'd it go with Xander last night?"

Of course Maggie knew he hadn't come back to the café.

"He wants another chance."

"Are you going to give it to him?"

Keisha shrugged. "I don't really know." Because her aunt's

words about the tax fees had wormed their way into her brain, and she couldn't stop thinking about it. He'd walked away from her for a few thousand dollars the last time, and this was potentially much more when considering profit he could make for selling the house. And she still really didn't know if his story was completely true.

"You'll know when you know," Maggie said, squeezing her arm. "For now, better get out there and start taking orders. I'm glad Cora didn't have school and that Garth pitched in for breakfast, or we would have had lines out the door. Don't worry about making butter cakes. I couldn't sleep last night and already made enough for the festival."

"That was a gamble."

Maggie grinned. "Not much. Dementia or no, Fletcher Wilson knows the weather."

The mention of Fletcher made Keisha frowned. "Any news from Ronica?"

"Not yet. I'm sure she'll call as soon as she has something to tell. Or as soon as she's ready." Meaning, of course, if Fletcher passed away.

Keisha pasted on a smile and went out to the counter to help Cora take orders. The teen turned from the cash register and gave her a weary smile, perspiration beading on her forehead. "I'm so glad you're here. I didn't even have time to comb my hair this morning." The long mass of brown was pulled into a decidedly messy ponytail, but it didn't really look different from any other day. Having difficult hair herself, Keisha understood the dilemma.

"I think you look great. Is your dress all finished?"

"Yep. Last night. And I've learned the songs." Cora beamed. "I'm going with Thom and Ingrid's wagon." Ingrid was another teen employee at the café, and Thom was her older brother and Cora's crush. "Thom's going to teach me to drive the wagon. It'll be like I'm a real pioneer." Cora turned back to a waiting customer. "Good morning. What will you have?"

"Who's next?" Keisha called.

The pre-lunch rush turned into the lunch rush, but when the power came back on at one, the crowd thinned. Cora went upstairs for a shower, and Keisha began prepping vegetables for dinner.

Mid-afternoon slowed enough for Keisha to zip home to dry her clothes, and after she began calling booth volunteers in between serving customers. She had some cancellations, but she was able to fill those by asking people to do double duty. Everyone seemed willing to help.

Xander showed up at the café when she was nearly finished, his arms full of bags and a big grin on his face. "This woodworking stuff Ronica arranged is awesome," he said. "Look. Birdhouses, bookends, money banks, and even a toolbox. And there are little aprons too. Simple construction with nails and hammers, and even some paint and stickers to decorate."

Keisha couldn't help smiling at his enthusiasm.

"My sisters will love it. Or at least Sammy will. The face painting is more Lila's speed."

Keisha laughed. "They'll probably like both."

"Probably. And all the volunteers are solid. In fact, I got Ernie and his son to take turns manning the woodworking booth. Ronica was going to have it basically self-serve with only a couple ladies from the knitting club there to hand out kits, but I wondered if all the moms and dads would have time to help the kids. Especially if they're overseeing other booths or participating in one of the competitions."

"Good thinking. Ernie will love that."

"I thought so, and the teens for the soda toss booth seem solid. Thom and Ingrid Patterson. You know them?"

"Oh, yeah, they're super responsible. In fact, Ingrid works here on weekends and some afternoons. She'll be in soon."

"Oh, good. I'll be sure to say hi." He paused a few seconds before saying. "What about you? How did it go with your aunt?"

Keisha's enthusiasm dipped a notch. Was he asking about the taxes or about her success in getting Olivia's help with the booths? "She's agreed to take over the face painting."

"That's good then. What about your other booths?"

"Almost booked up. I just need to fill two more half-hour slots for the dunking booth."

"Aw, and I was hoping it was the kissing booth you'd have to fill in for."

She laughed but couldn't help the rush of excitement rolling through her. "Keep dreaming."

He held her gaze a little too long. "Well, I'd better get these to Ernie. He wants to build a few to put on display so the kids will have examples to copy. I only stopped by to give you a report. I know you're worried about making sure the booths are ready."

Strangely, she hadn't been worried about his booths. He said he'd take care of it, and she trusted him.

Not a good thing.

Or maybe it was.

Before she could decide one way or the other, he added, "And okay, I'll take the slots at your dunking booth, but only if you promise not to dunk me." He waved and headed back outside.

Maggie came from the kitchen. "That was cute, him coming to get your approval."

"He wasn't—" But that was exactly what he'd been doing.

Maggie waved her protest aside. "It's what we all do. Seek approval from those we care about."

Maybe. Still, the fact that he'd wanted her to talk to Olivia about the fees weighed on her, even if it should have been a simple request between friends or acquaintances. As they were certainly not either of those things, it did matter.

Or was she making too much of nothing?

Maggie had said she would know, but Keisha had once known everything where Xander was concerned, and she'd been wrong. Could she trust herself again?

Maybe. She really wanted to.

CHAPTER 15

Friday evening, Xander met his mother and the twins for a picnic dinner at the park next to the café. The girls were already wearing their pioneer dresses, and even Sammy seemed content with the frills. They chased each other around the park, screaming and shouting.

Xander set down the fork he was using to eat one of Maggie's delicious takeout meals. He knew from experience that he should enjoy every second of it because the next weeks and months—and four years, really—were going to be filled with work and little time for home-cooked meals.

"I went through the house this morning," he said to his mother. "I didn't find anything that says grandpa was going to leave me the house. It looks like I'm going to have to apply for another loan. I guess it's only fair. We do owe the money."

His mother frowned. "It's my fault. I lost your inheritance. I'm really sorry."

"It's okay." He laid a hand on his mother's shoulder. She looked pale and weak but happy. "In ten years, it'll be a memory we'll laugh about."

"It could be in my storage at home, but I did look last week before you got here. He used to keep everything in a little wood box he made. Didn't you see anything like that at the house?"

He blinked. "Yeah, actually, and we took it that first night. Or rather, Sammy did. I told her she could have it. I think she put it in the bag you brought for her. But all that was in it were some old letters, clippings, and a few certificates. Didn't you see it?"

"No." Her face had brightened. "How thoroughly did you look through the papers? It's got to be in there."

They rounded up the girls and hurried back to her friend's house, where Sammy reluctantly handed over the box. Inside, there were only a few rocks.

"Sammy, where did the papers go?"

She shrugged. "I don't remember. It was just old junk. Maybe in the garbage?"

Their mother grabbed her shoulders. "Try to remember. Was it at the café? Here?"

"I think the café," Lila said helpfully. "Because it was empty when we found the rocks here yesterday."

A sinking sensation filled Xander's chest. "I'll go look," he told his mother, who was looking pale. "You should lie down."

"I'm sorry," she murmured.

"Can we come with you?" Sammy asked. "We can help look."

"Sure." He agreed more for his mother's welfare than for any "help" the girls might offer.

He drove back to the café, but the garbage in the room had been emptied even though he'd chosen the self-cleaning option that made the room less expensive. With a sigh, he sat on the bed.

"Well, it probably wasn't there anyway, but those were Grandpa's papers. I wish you'd asked before you threw them away."

"Wait!" Sammy's face broke into a smile. "I remember now. I put them in the drawer." She ran to the bottom drawer and tugged on it. Sure enough, the papers were haphazardly spread out over the drawer.

"Good job," he said, gathering the papers and setting them on the bed. "Look for anything handwritten, printed, or anything that says 'will.' It won't be a certificate or a newspaper clipping."

"We don't know how to read yet," Lila informed him. "Only really tiny words."

"Will is easy." He showed them how to spell it on his phone. "Also, look for my name or your mom's. You know how those are spelled, right?"

"Duh," Sammy said. He showed them anyway, leaving the phone turned on so they could double-check.

In silence, they began combing through the collection, making separate stacks of certificates, clippings, receipts, and letters.

When they were two-thirds through, Sammy held up a letter. "Ah, look, it's a letter to you," she said, holding out a sealed envelope.

"I didn't see that before."

"It was inside another envelope with Mom's name." Sammy passed over a larger envelope. "Will you read both to me?"

"Yeah, in a minute." Xander took out his pocketknife and carefully slit open the letter. Why had he never been given this? His eyes scanned the letter quickly. It detailed his grandfather's lung disease that had affected his blood vessels, as well as his love for Xander and his sorrow that he wouldn't be around to see him become a man. Also there, in black-and-white, was exactly what

Xander needed. His grandfather had left the house to him, not
to his mother as everyone assumed, which meant the city had
notified the wrong person about the taxes. This was what he
needed to convince the city to work with him.

The final words his grandfather wrote made him choke up.
*Xander, you have been the son I never had, and I am so proud of
you. You are a hard worker, and you are kind to others. You respect
and care for your mother. That is what life is about. I know I won't
live to see you grown, but I have all confidence that you will become
a man I will also be proud of. Love, Grandpa.*

"Xander, why are you crying?" Lila asked, her little face drawn
in concern.

"I'm not crying." He dropped the letter and reached out to
tickle both girls. "What do you think I am, a sissy?" They both
giggled and bounced out of the way.

He scooped everything up into a stack and tucked it under his
arm. "Come on, let's get you two back to Mom. We have a big
day tomorrow."

Tomorrow, the day Xander would take every opportunity to
be with Keisha and convince her that she could love him again.

"Wait," Sammy said, her hands on her little hips. "I am not
going yet. You said you would read us the letters."

"Okay, okay." So he did.

CHAPTER 16

The late-morning Harvest Festival gathering parade on Saturday morning went smoothly. Keisha had been assigned to the cart of a young and upcoming attorney instead of driving with her young cousin and her uncle the way she usually did. It was Olivia's not-so-subtle hint about her future, but it was fun anyway. Besides, she was so busy picking up baskets and boxes and sacks of food that she barely had time to talk with the man. All up and down Main Street, drivers and gatherers dressed in pioneer clothing sang the traditional harvest songs. If they were a bit out of tune, they made up for it with volume and enthusiasm.

By the time Keisha and the attorney reached the fairgrounds at the northern end of Main Street, their horse-drawn wagon was full of corn, wheat, soybeans, apples, grapes, berries, and every vegetable imaginable. Olivia met them there in her tailored pioneer garb, a bright turquoise piece that made Keisha's patterned dress look like it came from a bargain basement, which it had. Olivia directed the unloading into large canopy tents that were as white and pristine as her kitchen.

The sun blazed over the fairgrounds, already bustling with celebrants. The heat yesterday and today had dried out much of the earth, making the wood planks laid down yesterday in the booth areas unnecessary, though Keisha was happy about the notable lack of dust that sometimes plagued the area during past festivals. The board walkway and the pioneer costumes gave Keisha the feeling of having transported back to the time when Chelsea and James Morgan settled the town. No one seemed to mind the heat, and some enterprising teens had even set up a makeshift booth of tiny spray bottles filled with water and ice, which were selling faster than Maggie's butter cakes.

Keisha stopped to watch a group of young girls making corn-husk dolls from the husks Maggie had collected this week from the community and saved in one of her large refrigerators. Keisha had once kept a collection of the dolls she'd made over the years, but they burned up with her parents' house. Seeing them now made her both happy and sad in a nostalgic way.

Next, she stopped to watch a group of men playing tug of war over a huge hole in the ground layered with thick black plastic and filled with water. Years ago, they'd used a small, muddy ditch, but the hole had grown over the years. The rope had grown too, now fifty feet long and as thick as Keisha's wrist, with big knots in it where groups of mostly men, but some women and children too, would grip it in the attempt to make others take the plunge. The water in the hole today was warm and only a little dirty—Keisha had checked it earlier while setting up her booth—but by the end of the day, it would be filthy as little boys and men tossed dirt into it to challenge their opponents.

The men finished their war, five from one side being pulled

into the water, at which point, all the others on their team let go. Good-natured groans filled the air. Keisha laughed to see Xander hop out of the water with a couple of guys she'd known in high school, grins on their faces as they slapped him on the back.

Spying her, he hurried over. "Something tells me it was a setup," he said, looking down at his pants, now wet past the knees. "Those guys were definitely not trying."

She grinned. "They always initiate the newcomers, and since you've been gone so long, this is their way of welcoming you back."

"I should have known when they couldn't hold against all those old farts. Seriously."

She laughed again, wiping the beads of perspiration from her forehead with her fingertips. "Well, next year you can do it to someone else." Belatedly, she realized the words assumed he would stay and that he wouldn't simply leave for greener pastures.

"I mean," she began hurriedly, but Cora appeared at her elbow, looking adorable in her blue, homemade pioneer dress, white apron, and matching bonnet that now lay loosely down her back.

"I am so sorry, Keisha," she said, "but my dad won't let me take the shift at the kissing booth. And neither will Ingrid's dad, even though she got someone to cover for her at the soda toss so she could do it with me." The teen's lip stuck out in a pout. "I told Dad it would only be on the cheek, and Maggie also tried to tell him it was okay, but he said no way and that he knows from personal experience what a kiss could lead to." She sighed and rolled her eyes in a decidedly practiced manner. "How will I ever get a kiss from Thom now? I swear he's shyer than a newborn colt."

Keisha put an arm around the girl. "You don't need a kissing booth for that. Believe me. It will happen when it's supposed to. Don't be in a rush."

"But I'm seventeen already. I'm like super old not to be kissed."

"Not in Forgotten, you're not," Keisha assured her. "Because here it really means something. Remember when I told you that at the Spring Planting Dance, couples who kiss at midnight stay together forever?"

Cora put her hands on her hips. "Yeah, right. Laina says she's kissed five or something guys there, and it never stuck." She tossed her head. "Oh, never mind, I'll just go to the soda toss after I help Maggie sell butter cakes. At least I can *talk* to Thom without my dad having a fit. But why even have a kissing booth if no one thinks we should be kissing?" She stalked off, looking disgusted.

Keisha met Xander's gaze. A subtle tension that hadn't been there before crept between them. "So," he said a little too casually, "looks like you'll be at the kissing booth after all. You sure you don't want me to buy up all your kisses so you don't get any weirdos?"

Keisha rolled her eyes, ignoring the abrupt pounding of her heart. "Xander."

He shrugged. "You can't blame a guy for trying."

"Right." She gave him a smile that told him she wasn't going to let it worry her. And she wouldn't because, in truth, it was better that he'd said something than if he hadn't, which was silly and stupid, and a totally inappropriate thing to feel when she'd been the one who warned him to back off.

"Well," she added hastily, "I'd better go round up some replacements for their shift. I knew I should have talked to their parents first." With a wave and not quite meeting his gaze, she gathered her skirts and hurried away.

She searched the growing crowd for anyone she knew more than by casual acquaintance. Her eyes landed on Laina. Dressed in a bright red dress with a tiny feathered cap, she was stunning, standing like a beacon in the array of tame pioneer grays, browns, and blues. Today, instead of her hair being its usual frizz, she'd curled it in large waves.

Ah, Laina would do nicely, and with her was . . . no, she couldn't ask Jeremy Wilson to volunteer at the kissing booth, or he might read something into it. What was he doing here anyway when his father was in the hospital?"

Keisha hurried over to the couple, and Laina grinned as she spied her. "Guess what? Fletcher's going to be okay."

"Really?" Keisha felt an unexpected rush of warmth in her chest.

Jeremy nodded, pushing his cowboy hat back onto his head. "That's right, and as soon as my mom got the news this morning, she sent me home to help with set up. Everyone had it mostly done, but she wanted a report."

Laina rolled her eyes. "My mother has been on the phone with Ronica all morning, taking down her orders. She should relax a bit and focus on your dad."

"If you ask me," Jeremy said with a grin, "she's probably eaten alive with jealousy that you're pulling this off without her."

"Probably," Laina agreed.

Keisha laughed. "Well, we really couldn't have done it without all her planning. Anyway, I'm happy for you and your mom." She patted his arm a bit awkwardly because they were friends, even if he didn't get the hint that she didn't want to date him.

"Thanks," he said. "Guess I'll go give Mom an update. If it's okay, I'll tell her everyone is crazy without her but making it work."

"That would be the truth," Laina said with a laugh. "She makes it look so easy."

Keisha turned to Laina as Jeremy moved off. "Look, are you doing anything at six? I need a little help."

"Sure. I've got a break between one and three, and five and seven, actually. Mom insisted, or she was going to put her foot down about me even coming. And this is the first year I get to play Chelsea Morgan in the play. I barely convinced her to let me continue."

"Right, I almost forgot about that." Laina had been chosen to play Chelsea Morgan, likely the reason for the tamer hair and red dress, which had been Chelsea's favorite color, though Laina probably would have worn the dress anyway.

Laina gave an exaggerated sigh. "Seriously, how old do you have to be to be an adult in this town?"

"I think it has something to do with having kids," Keisha said.

Laina snorted a laugh. "You got that right, but my mom apparently hasn't gotten the message where Trish is concerned. She's got three kids now, and Mom still checks on how she separates her laundry."

"Whoa, when did that happen? Not the laundry, but the three kids." Keisha knew Laina's older sister was married and had a baby, but there were three already? "Crazy."

"I know. But what is it you need? I hope it's something I can do with my arm in this cast." She raised her arm with the bright red sling that Keisha was sure Doc hadn't given her.

"Well, you see, Cora and Ingrid just quit at one of my booths, and I need two fill-ins." Keisha made a face but added quickly, "Not that it's their fault. "It was a parental decision. But it's definitely something you can do with only one arm."

"Sure. Which booth?"

Keisha hesitated before responding. "The kissing booth," she said, her voice sheepish.

"No way. I am done kissing old frogs or hormonal teens. But I'll help you find replacements. Shouldn't be too hard."

"Thanks."

"Let's meet back here in about fifteen minutes. I'm sure that's all it will take."

But when they met back up not fifteen minutes but an hour later, neither of them had found a single volunteer.

Laina made a face. "You know what this means, right?"

Keisha nodded. "We shut down the booth an hour early."

"No, no, no, no!" Laina shook her head. "We can't let Ronica down. She's counting on us to make this the best Harvest Festival ever."

"It's only an hour, and everyone will be going over to the reenactment at seven anyway."

Laina's expression sobered. "Ronica has always been there for this town. Now it's our turn."

That was certainly true, and the city did need the money for drainage on the road to Panna Creek.

"So what this means is I'll have to fill in," Laina continued. "Or rather, *we* will have to fill in. Because I'm not doing it alone."

Keisha's mind immediately strayed to Xander. "You gotta be kidding." She didn't know if she hoped Xander heard about it, or if she would rather him stay far, far away.

"Nope. We're doing this."

"Fine," she said, resignation and defeat—and maybe just a little bit of excitement?—in her voice. "Meet you there at six."

Next, Keisha hurried off to Maggie's bread booth. Maggie and Garth had constructed an outdoor oven, and though they'd tested it, Keisha was anxious to see how it was working out. Then she'd check on all her booths again. She set off, the patterned gingham of her pioneer dress swishing at her ankles.

She was biting into a thick slab of fresh bread dripping with butter when Xander appeared at her side, his hands in his back pockets. His two sisters were next to him, each carrying a bag full of what looked like projects and winnings from the booths. "Hey," she said, licking the butter from her lips.

His eyes followed the motion, stirring unexpected heat inside her. "Just wanted to report that my booths are running well. Old Ernest is improving on the birdhouse model. He brought wood and saws."

"Let me guess—all the tools are borrowed and the supplies donated by the local hardware store."

"That and salvaged from the pasta factory construction site. The new home sites too."

She laughed. "Why am I not surprised?" She looked at the girls. "Was it fun?"

"The best ever!" Sammy said while Lila nodded vigorously.

"Want a piece of bread?" Keisha asked. "It's made in ovens just like the pioneers used to have."

"I do, I do." The girls chimed together.

"We'll take three," Xander said. "How much?"

Maggie turned from the table and handed them each a paper plate with a slice of bread. "No charge for those who run the booths or for cute little twins."

Xander took his plate with one hand as the girls went to sit on one of Maggie's coolers. "Thanks, Maggie," he said. But he didn't bite into the bread, and his other hand was still awkwardly behind his back. When Maggie smiled and turned away, he stepped closer to Keisha and said in a low voice, "I have something for you."

She blinked as he pulled his other hand from behind his back. In it was a cornhusk doll whose skirt had been dyed a bright, still-drying red. He pushed it into her free hand. "Um, I took the girls to the booth, and I remember you telling me about those you'd lost . . . uh, in the fire. So now you have another one to begin a new collection." He made a face. "It's supposed to be Chelsea Morgan, but now that I look at it, it seems to remind me more of Laina. You see these tiny curled husk pieces mixed in with cornsilk? They're supposed to be—"

"Chelsea's hair." Emotion welled up inside her. The first cornhusk doll she'd ever made was of Chelsea Morgan. The fact that he'd remembered made her feel off balance, as if she had missed something important along the line. "Thanks," she choked out.

He set his plate on a nearby table and held up red-dyed fingertips. "I'm afraid I got food coloring on my fingers just like you when you made your original doll. I hope it fades a bit before I go to the hospital on Monday. I'm pretty sure it's not a plus to have a new resident go around looking like they have bloodstains on their hands." He wiggled his fingers as if they were worms.

Laughter bubbled up inside her, which she understood was his intention. "Ha, you're a doctor, and no one questions them wearing gloves. But really, a little vinegar and soda should remove it. And I love the doll. Thank you so much. You can't know what it means to me."

"Well, I can't tell you how much it means to have my grandfather's collection of cars, so maybe do I understand a little."

She smiled at him. "Maybe so."

"Though I know losing him wasn't the same thing as losing your parents," he added hurriedly, his eyes intent on her face.

She nodded, letting the old sadness well up and through her in a rush. It was better to let it come and then let it go rather than trying to push it away as she'd been doing to her feelings for Xander for the past four and a half years. That just made the loss fester and hurt more.

The sadness dissipated as it always did. Silence grew between them, not awkward but expectant. She wanted to hug him and tell him she was glad he'd come back to Forgotten . . . yet she couldn't. But perhaps she was one step closer.

"Well," he said with a smile that showed no hint of sadness though it wasn't his full smile. "I'll take the girls back to my mother and get to cracking the whip over my booths. It's kind of fun being in charge." With a wink, he picked up his plate and called the girls before he faded into the crowd, leaving her to stare after him.

CHAPTER 17

Xander watched Jeremy Wilson throw a ring over one of the tallest two-liter soda bottles, winning his second bottle. With three bottles, he could trade them in for a small stuffed animal. Xander was secretly proud of the set up. Instead of a boring bowling pin layout, he'd stacked wood and borrowed a few tables from his dad's workshop to create differing heights for the soda bottles. The design spiraled upwards in a rough DNA pattern, though no one except him would even guess at it.

Jeremy made another toss and missed. "Shoot," he said. "I need to win that little cat."

The freckled girl, Ingrid, laughed. "Winning that cat, cute as it is, isn't going to make Keisha go out with you."

"You never know." Jeremy handed over another dollar. He had a badge pinned on him for winning the hay bale toss, which he'd apparently been champion of for the last three years. Xander had been tempted to join the contest, but though they could use gloves, his hands were already a bit torn up from the tug-of-war, which wasn't good for his first day at work. Besides, he knew when to cut his losses. If ever there was a man built for tossing hay bales, it was Jeremy Wilson, who had been farming all his life.

Ingrid wrinkled her nose, making her freckles run together. "I do know. Keisha won't be won by a plush toy. Maybe no one can win her. I think the love of her life died a mysterious death, and her heart is broken, never to heal again." Ingrid put her hand over her heart like a real pioneer girl acting in a school play.

Jeremy shook his head. "Keisha has a lot more sense than to waste her entire life mourning a dead man. You'll see. She's one of the strongest women I know, next to my mom. She's just had a few rough years with the accident and all."

Xander agreed with everything he said, and it rankled him that Jeremy understood so much about Keisha, but then he'd been here these past four years while Xander had been missing in action.

"I guess you're right," Ingrid said. "I mean, she runs the café without a hiccup when Maggie's gone, and Maggie always depends on her to do this or that. Not sure what will happen when she moves on." She shot a pointed glance in Xander's direction. "Maybe what Keisha needs right now isn't more boring online classes but something new and mysterious."

"Who needs something new and mysterious?" Cora appeared at Xander's elbow. "Because if it's me you're talking about, then yes, I do." Her smile was all for Ingrid's brother, Thom, who readily smiled back.

"We were talking about Keisha," Ingrid said.

"Oh. Dad says she'll be running this city after her uncle steps down."

"I could see that." Ingrid grinned. "But speaking of Keisha, did she find anyone to cover our shift at the kissing booth?"

Cora giggled, sneaking a peek at Thom. "I just asked, and nope. She and Laina are going to fill in themselves."

That caught not only Xander's but Jeremy's attention. "What time was your shift?" Jeremy asked.

"Six o'clock," Ingrid said. "Right before the reenactment. Laina's going to play Chelsea this year, you know. That's why she's wearing red."

"She'd probably be wearing it anyway," Cora added. "Wish I dared to do color like she does."

"She's a little too bright if you ask me." Jeremy tossed his final ring, and it slid easily over one of the bottles. "Yes!" he exclaimed, punching a fist into the air. "I'll take that cat now, and at six, you'll know where to find me." The girls laughed as he kissed the cat in his big hands and walked away.

Xander's irritation grew. Why had he agreed to the no-kissing thing? Well, it didn't matter. He was going over to that booth *before* six to buy up all Keisha's kissing slots. How many could there be? Even if she wouldn't kiss him, he'd make darn sure she wasn't kissing Jeremy Wilson.

Even as he had the thought, he felt guilty. She was a grown woman and could take care of herself. He had no rights here—except that he hadn't left her on purpose. Yet he had taken the easy way out four years ago; he saw that now. Youth had been his only excuse.

Never again.

"I'll be back later," he said, turning away.

"Aren't you supposed to be at the dunking booth?" Thom asked.

Xander checked his watch. Sure enough, it was past four-thirty, which meant he was late for the first of his half-hour shifts. The commitment would cut short his time to plan, but maybe Keisha would come to dunk him, and he could talk to her then. Would she laugh if she knew how the idea of her kissing Jeremy tore him up inside? Would he even tell her? He was sure it wasn't the manly thing to do, but he'd play it by ear.

The elderly lady running the dunking booth somehow managed to round up a gaggle of excited high school girls to pay good money to dunk the hometown boy turned doctor. On top of that, the old woman triggered the last dunk herself by hitting the target with her hand after his replacement appeared at five-thirty. So after six dunks, Xander climbed out of the dunking booth, wondering why Keisha had missed the opportunity to douse him. Had she run into an issue with one of her other booths?

He still had nearly thirty minutes before Keisha would be at the kissing booth, but he'd better hurry if he was to put his plan into action and head Jeremy off. He felt the water drying on his hot skin just thinking about it.

He started for the bathrooms to change but came up short when Olivia Campbell stepped into his path. He caught himself from trampling her and stared, aware of his hair plastered against his head and the water dripping down his pants into his newly donned sneakers.

He ran a hand through his hair self-consciously. "Good afternoon," he said with a nod. He had already talked to Penny about getting the new information about his grandfather's house and his stated intention to live in the house to the city council on Monday, but maybe braving the dragon now could fast-forward the result.

"Is it? That depends."

He gazed around, puzzled. "Well, it's a little hot, I guess. Taking a turn in the dunking booth cooled me right off."

Olivia's lips pursed in disapproval. "How much will it take to make you go away this time?"

He blinked at her. "I don't know what you're talking about."

"Is it your grandfather's house? The tax penalties?" Olivia put her hands on her hips, now covered by a svelte emerald pioneer dress that looked as if it cost as much as his house. "I'll make them waive the fees if you agree to sell the house and leave town. Or I'll even pay you extra for the house if you abandon your plan to take it back. The way I see it, you and your mother forfeited your rights when you left this town and everything in the house."

His urge to tell her about his grandfather's written will died on his lips. "That's not the way it works, and you know it."

"What I know is that you hurt my niece, and now you're back to do it again."

The accusation felt like a stab to the heart, one he likely deserved, but the woman standing before him wasn't without culpability. The words she used told him she knew of Keisha's suffering and had allowed it to continue. Even if Keisha decided not to come back to him, Xander would not abandon her to this wolf in women's clothing.

"No," he growled. "I came for her, and *you* convinced me she didn't want to see me, that she sent you to tell me to go away." He clenched his teeth to stem his anger before continuing. "Back then, I knew I wasn't good enough for her or you, and maybe that's why I was convinced, but I've proven myself since." But standing dripping wet in front of her, he suddenly didn't feel good enough, as if he were still the white piece of trash she deemed too lowly for her niece.

"You've proven nothing." Her tone was sharp and acidic. "How do I know you're not just here to get your hands on the rest of Keisha's money?"

"What are you talking about? For the record, as far as I understand it, you're the one trying to control her with money. I don't need her money, and I don't want any from you. I can take care of my own finances."

"You mean like you did the last time?" Olivia's smirk drilled into him.

His hands clenched at his sides. "That was a mistake. And believe me, I intend to pay you back every cent now that I understand what it was you were doing." He leaned toward her, his gaze piercing hers. "Losing Keisha was the worst thing that ever happened to me. *To us.* I loved her. I *still* love her, and I would give up everything—*everything*—I've accomplished since to go back and make sure she never came home to tell you about our plans. To make that accident never happen. I don't care if you don't waive the tax penalties, even though I have evidence that it's my house, not my mother's, and I was never notified. I also don't care if I go into debt for the rest of my life. I'm not going anywhere unless Keisha herself tells me to."

Olivia laughed. "Be that as it may, you will not have her—I'll make sure of that." With a flounce that was entirely in keeping with her elaborate costume, she turned and sauntered away, the fancy hat on her upswept hair teetering dangerously on her head.

Xander stared at her retreating back for a long minute, tortured by the same old emotions that had made him retreat four years ago. Then, he shook his head. "No," he said softly, and then more loudly and resolutely, "No freaking way."

It was enough to jolt him out of his shock. He wasn't going to let that woman come between him and Keisha. Not again. Not ever. He glanced at his phone. There was no time to change now. He'd jog to his truck and then fight for Keisha, no matter how embarrassing it might be for both of them. He couldn't stand by and do nothing while another man courted the woman he loved.

It might be his last chance.

CHAPTER 18

Keisha came up short as she spied Olivia and Xander between the dunking booth and the cornhusk dolls, not toward the front near the walk but at the back where no one was likely to bother them. Olivia was talking, her hands on her hips, while Xander stood there dripping wet. Someone must have dunked him, and she regretted not being the one, but she'd been literally roped into a tug of war between the single women of the town and the married ones. Fortunately, her team won, though the other team let go before falling into the now-muddy water. No one wanted to ruin the pioneer dresses they'd worked so hard on.

Keisha moved closer to the pair, but Olivia was already walking off, and Xander, looking frustrated, stalked away as well without a glance in her direction. What had they been talking about? The taxes on his house? Keisha tasted bile in her throat.

Olivia's gaze met hers, a smile coming to her face. "Keisha, dear," she said, closing the space between them, "have you had time to stop at the face painting booth? You'll be impressed with what I've come up with." She said this last in sing song.

"I saw it," Keisha said. As expected, her aunt had gone overboard with the preparations. "Where did you get the artists?"

"Oh, a friend of mine brought them down from Lincoln."

Keisha lifted her gaze to the spot where Xander had disappeared. Should she ask her aunt what they'd been discussing? Somehow, she was sure she already knew.

"Look, dear," Olivia said, glancing in the same direction, "I don't like how we left things this morning. Family is always the most important thing, and we can't let that boy come between us. And I must say that the more I talk to him, the more grateful I am that things didn't work out between you two. You dodged a bullet. He's not what he pretends to be. Even just now, he was asserting that his grandfather left the house to him, not to his mother, so he hadn't been properly notified about the back taxes. That's how far he'll go to cheat our town."

Something in her tone rang false—classic Olivia. Keisha's ire flared. "If you want to discuss Xander, let's talk about the day he came to see you while I was in the hospital after my accident. Was that at the house?"

"Uh . . . y-yes." Olivia had obviously realized there was no denying the visit. "Where else would it be?" Her words were clipped and quiet. "But, please, keep your voice down." She flicked her gaze pointedly toward the cornhusk booth behind her.

Keisha ignored the warning. "It could have been at the hospital. Didn't you tell him where I was?"

"Does it matter?"

"Yes, it matters." Suddenly, it mattered a lot. If Xander had really thought she left him, maybe the rest of his story and intentions were true. Which would mean it hadn't been his neglect or fate or a rainy night that cruelly ripped them apart, but Olivia.

"When you gave me my new phone, there were no calls from him," Keisha said. Her original phone had been ruined in the accident, or so she was told, but Olivia kindly purchased her a new one from the education fund her parents left for her. The fact that Xander never contacted her had hurt deeply. She nearly called his number dozens of times over the next few months, but each time, she disconnected before finishing, believing he didn't deserve her devotion. "Did you delete them?"

"There were a few that came through." Olivia waved a hand dismissively. "But since he already promised to stay away . . ."

"You deleted them." And Keisha had stupidly believed her aunt when she said there had been no word. "Did you also block his number?"

Olivia's mouth tightened. "Trust me. You were better off." Her gaze dropped to the shiny new boots poking from underneath her dress, where a smudge of dirt must be driving her crazy.

"I *loved* him," Keisha responded. "So much." The reality struck hard. "You stole that from me. You stole all my plans and took away my choices. You took advantage of my trust."

Yet Keisha understood that she alone was really to blame, not her aunt. She'd let hurt keep her from Xander—that was the bottom-line truth she had to live with for the rest of her life. It was why it had taken her so long to move on. She knew she hadn't really tried.

"He was everything to me," she went on, choking with emotion. "And without him . . . well, can you even begin to realize how long it took me to want to live without Xander? He made me happy again after my parents died, and you almost killed me. That's what you did." The painful memories threatened to crush her.

"You were better off." Olivia sounded less sure now. She looked entirely pretentious at that moment in her extravagant dress with her elaborate wig and artfully made-up face.

"No," Keisha shot back. "I wasn't. What you did was outright lie, and I don't think I can ever forgive you." She started to turn away, to run after Xander to tell him she believed his story now. What if it was too late? What if Olivia had sewn more poison between them? She should have wrapped her arms around him in her kitchen when she'd had the chance. A sense of urgency spread through her.

"Keisha!" Olivia's voice rose an octave, carrying to the cornhusk doll booth where the participants looked over at them, eager for gossip. Olivia's voice lowered as she added, "How can you say that after everything I've done for you?"

Keisha faced her again, arms folded across her abdomen, an outward sign of protection. "You will approve Xander's request about his tax penalties," she said quietly, "or I'll never speak to or see you again." She didn't want to see Olivia anyway, but she would for Charlie's sake—and for Xander's. But only if Olivia did this for her.

"Because whatever you do," Keisha continued, "I'm giving Xander a second chance. And I'm going to stay in Forgotten and help build this town. I'm going to ensure that what makes us unique thrives while we grow. In five years, your control over me will end. Your emotional control is already over. It's your choice if you want to be a part of my life or not, but I am the only one who will make my decisions from here on out. Me. Not you."

Olivia's mouth worked, as if trying to form a reply, but before she could make an intelligent response, Keisha walked away, unhurried and resolute. She sucked in a steadying breath. No matter how terribly her emotions raged within, she'd been strong, not hysterical or out of control. Distanced calm was the language Olivia spoke best. Now she'd either do what Keisha asked or not. Either way, Keisha knew what she had to do.

Keisha didn't find Xander in either of his booths or near the food stands, and she couldn't find his truck in the parking lot or where cars spilled out onto the street. Surely he had to be here somewhere. Had he gone to the restrooms to change his wet clothing? Or maybe he'd forgotten to bring a change and had to run back to the Butter Cake. An uneasiness stirred within her.

Maybe he'd cut out altogether.

No, that was Olivia in her head, and she wouldn't give in to those insecurities. She'd been through too much to take offense at anything but a face-to-face rejection from Xander. She did another quick round at his booths without success before deciding she had no choice but to call off her search and head to the stupid kissing booth, which she'd make sure wasn't part of the Harvest Festival next year, no matter what Ronica said. Instead, they'd auction off movie tickets or an hour of farm work. She knew farmers who would pay a lot more than a buck for that, but somehow she'd turn the money into a way to attract a hospital to Forgotten. They needed it with the new pasta factory and the people it would bring. She would turn her economic studies into a good cause for the town—her town. Her uncle and Doc would help, and maybe even Xander.

She'd nearly reached the kissing booth and was surprised to find a small crowd that included not only Xander but also Cora, Ingrid, Jeremy Wilson, and two retired old-timers, Larry

and Sam. The high school girl and the young divorcee she and
Laina were supposed to relieve were still behind the counter,
and Laina was with them. They were all staring at a paper on
the table that marked the separation between the booth workers
and customers. A pile of dollar bills lay on the counter next to
the clipboard.

"That's ridiculous," Jeremy said. "There's never a sign-up sheet.
There's just a line. There's always just a line."

"I don't know," said Larry, the old-timer with receding white
hair and a penchant for extra cream in his coffee. He shoved
himself between Jeremy and Xander to grab a pen. "Looks like
there's a sign up to me." He scribbled something—under Laina's
name, Keisha saw, because all the fifty slots under her own name
were filled.

Laina accepted a dollar bill from Larry and gave him a kiss
on the cheek. The man laughed, flushing a deep red. "Thankee,
Laina. Yer a real sweet doll."

"Right back at you," she said with a wink. "And you know it's
for a good cause."

"That's why I'm here."

"No," said his best buddy Sam. "It's because you ain't been
kissed in twenty years." He signed his own name and slapped a
buck down on the table. "Neither have I. If I pay double, do I
get it on the lips?"

"Only if you want to marry me," Laina teased.

Sam scratched at his full head of gray hair. "Guess I'm too old
for that." He presented his cheek.

As the two old-timers wandered off, Keisha slid behind the
table. No one else moved, but all eyes turned in her direction.

"I'll pay double for one of Keisha's slots," Jeremy said, glancing
over at her. In his hands, he was strangling a tiny stuffed cat.

"I already paid double—for every one of them." Xander looked so fierce that Keisha wanted to laugh, but somehow she managed to hold it in. Cora and Ingrid weren't as controlled, and their amused giggles filled the booth. Xander frowned at them and succeed only in making them laugher harder.

Two young boys came up and put down money. Laina groaned under her breath. "Remind me again why we agreed to this?"

"We didn't exactly," Keisha said.

"Tell him he can't do that." Jeremy glared at Xander as Laina gave each of the boys a kiss on the cheek.

"He already knows," Keisha said, but her eyes were locked on Xander, the familiar lines of his face echoing in her heart. He'd obviously changed since the dunking booth, and his combed hair was almost dry with the heat. "What are you doing?" she asked him.

"You said I had everything I need, but you're wrong. I don't have you." He leaned over the table and grabbed her hands. "I'd give up everything else to have you back in my life. It wouldn't matter if we were in some remote African jungle or here . . . farming." His gaze flicked briefly in Jeremy's direction and then back to her. "I never stopped loving you. You said you'd give me a chance, and I believe you. But right now that means I either buy all your kisses, and we stand here like this until the time's up, or you tell me to leave."

She understood then. He wasn't trying to break her rules. He was standing his ground despite whatever Olivia had said to him. He was showing her that he wasn't running, that he'd fight for her.

"Okay." Because she'd forgiven him already, and she was going to try to forgive herself.

Next to Xander, Ingrid squealed. "I knew it!"

"Laina's still open," Cora told Jeremy helpfully. "Come on. It's for a good cause."

Then, because Jeremy was a good sport, or maybe he already understood that he'd lost, he slapped down a five-dollar bill. "Okay, but here's five bucks because in that dress, Laina, I have to say, you look like a million."

"Why, thank you, Jeremy. Just for that, you get a real kiss." She glanced at Cora and Ingrid. "Girls, don't try this at home." She put both hands on the table and leaned over to kiss Jeremy, who met her halfway. His eyes opened wide as she kissed him fully on the lips.

Xander came around the table without releasing her hands, and Keisha stepped into his arms as if she'd been doing so every day for the past four and a half years. He hesitated, but she lifted her lips to his and kissed him. Not once but every one of the fifty kisses he'd paid for, as well as a couple more for good measure.

The kisses were most definitely not on the cheek.

"Where did you find all those ones anyway?" she asked him when they finally came up for air.

His lips twitched in a sardonic smile. "There's an ATM on Main, and Maggie was happy to break the hundred down from the money she's collected. I'm not totally destitute, you know."

"Of course not, but . . ."

He laughed. "Worth every cent."

For that, she kissed him again.

Later, as they walked hand in hand toward the reenactment behind a sarcastic Laina and an oddly dazed Jeremy, Keisha ran into her uncle and young cousin.

"Mom went home," Charlie announced. "I told her it was bad luck to miss the reenactment, but she didn't care. She's tired."

Josiah leaned in toward her. "Olivia told me what happened.

Good for you. And this time don't worry about your funds. When the time comes, I'll see that she approves of whoever you marry, or I'll be the one making her life difficult. Once before, I bowed to her despite my better judgment, but I won't do it again. I've also been informed about the city council's decision on Xander's house. She's in charge of housing, but I will get involved if she doesn't do the right thing. This town needs another doctor, and he's worth the investment." He smiled. "On both the personal and professional fronts."

"Thank you." Keisha hugged him. "I'm so lucky to have you."

Xander's twin sisters chose that moment to come running up behind him, throwing themselves into his arms. "We're set up over there," his mother said, pointing as she caught up to the girls. Her eyes went down to where her son's hand interlocked with Keisha's. "We have plenty of chairs, if you'd like to come. We set up late, so we're pretty far back, though." She laughed, as if knowing that right now their eyes would only be for each other.

Keisha returned her smile. "Thank you. I'd like that."

Saying goodbye to Josiah and Charlie, Xander and Keisha sat behind his mother's group of friends. They were far enough away from the makeshift stage that they could barely make out Laina in her red dress.

Xander scooted closer, a silly smile on his face, his arm around her. "Marry me," he whispered in her ear. "Anywhere, anytime."

A vision of the African jungle they'd talked about danced in her memories, but she had grown strong roots in this town. She had friends and family she loved, and his mother and sisters needed him.

"Let's do it in April like we always planned. I'll finish my degree by then, and you might have a week off."

"We could still elope to Africa."

She shook her head. "Maybe someday. Right now, I have everything I need right here."

His arms tightened around her, both stealing her breath and giving her reason to breathe. "Me too."

HISTORY OF FORGOTTEN
and James and Chelsea Morgan

In the late 1850s in Missouri, James Morgan, the son of a wealthy farmer, and Chelsea Fortson, the daughter of an important abolitionist cattle rancher, fell in love and wanted to marry, but their fathers were sworn enemies, divided on the issue of slavery, so they separated their children, forbidding them to associate or fall in love—as if such a thing could be mandated.

Not that their fathers didn't try. James was made to travel to Virginia, where his father, who had been elected to government office, moved in an attempt to influence the politicians there in favor of slavery. Chelsea was sent to what would eventually become Kansas to live with relatives, who, like Chelsea's father, were firmly on the side of Kansas entering the Union as a free state. For three years, James and Chelsea lived apart with nothing more than secret letters passed between them, aided by loyal friends and servants.

James worked hard managing one of his father's farms, and he eventually put together enough funds to get himself to Kansas to ask Chelsea to run away with him. He showed up on her door-step, his identity disguised, and she packed a bag and left with him that same night. When their marriage was discovered, both of them were disowned by their disgruntled families.

They thought that would be the end of their struggle, and their families would eventually come to accept their union. Unfortunately, they married in early 1861, near the same time Kansas was formed and became a free state. Embittered by his defeat, James's father considered his son's marriage an affront to his entire way of life, and it wasn't enough to simply disinherit James for his betrayal. Instead, he sent a posse after him, made up of the wildest, ferocious, and murderous men. They found James in Kansas and shot him. Chelsea, eight months pregnant with her first child, threw herself in front of him. Her beauty was such that these ruffians took pity on her and left him to bleed out in her arms.

Chelsea, accustomed to tending wounded cattle, stopped the bleeding and called for a doctor. James's leg had to be ampu-tated, and he nearly died of infection, but Chelsea slowly nursed him back to health, all the while keeping his survival a secret. She wrote to her father, begging for his help and forgiveness and telling him about his grandchild. Only years later did she learn that he'd died after being shot by his pro-slavery enemies. Her brother inherited their large ranch and, being a greedy man, tore up her letter so he wouldn't have to share.

When no help came, Chelsea earned a living making ravioli at a restaurant during the day and sewing dresses late into the night until James was finally well enough to come out of hiding. By then, they wanted nothing to do with their families, so they took off to the northern part of Kansas near the border of what would become Nebraska. They built a one-room cabin and began to farm. Thirteen children were born to them, and Chelsea often walked the fields at night with her children, hand-in-hand, teaching them the harvest songs.

When people passing through the area asked James and Chelsea where they were from, they claimed they'd been gone so long that they'd forgotten because they feared word might get back to their families. Most of the couple's thirteen children married people from nearby towns and returned to help farm the land. The town became known as Forgotten, a place of a new life for all those who had been or wanted to be forgotten, and where thirteen was the luckiest number.

To this day, weddings, birthdays, and other special events are always planned for the thirteenth. Every year in Forgotten, the town celebrates the first harvest by singing the harvest songs and reenacting the story of James and Chelsea Morgan with the hope that Chelsea will bless the harvest for another year.

Legend has it that people who stay in Forgotten, especially those running from their past or those who want to forget, usually end up finding themselves.

℟achel Branton has worked in publishing for over twenty years. She loves writing women's fiction and traveling, and she hopes to write and travel a lot more. As a mother of seven, it's not easy to find time to write, but the semi-ordered chaos gives her a constant source of writing material. She's been known to wear pajamas all day when working on a deadline, and is often distracted enough to burn dinner. (Okay, pretty much 90% of the time.) A sign on her office door reads: Danger. Enter at Your Own Risk. Writer at Work. Under the name Rachel Branton, she writes romance, romantic suspense, and women's fiction. Rachel also writes urban fantasy, paranormal romance, and science fiction under the name Teyla Branton. For more information or to sign up to hear about new releases, please visit www.RachelBranton.com.

Made in the USA
Las Vegas, NV
02 October 2021